The Closed Circle

by **CORINNE GERSON**

Cover illustration
by Lydia Rosier

SCHOLASTIC BOOK SERVICES
NEW YORK • TORONTO • LONDON • AUCKLAND • SYDNEY • TOKYO

This book is for Risa,
my very own little girl

ISBN 0-590-31792-X

Copyright © 1968 by Corinne Gerson. All rights
reserved. Published by Scholastic Book Services, a
Division of Scholastic Magazines, Inc., by arrange-
ment with the Author, Corinne Gerson.

12 11 10 9 8 7 6 5 4 3 2 1   10   0 1 2 3 4 5 / 8
Printed in the U. S. A.   06

chapter 1

Audrey tried out a horrible grin at her reflection in the mirror. She smoothed the shiny black folds of her long witch dress, and set the tall, pointed hat carefully on her head. It was a neat Halloween costume, she thought. Francine had cut out the dress and sewed it on Mom's machine and had helped her make the hat. And all those silver bats and cats and moons on the hat and dress had been glued on by Jimmy. Audrey herself had made the hideous mask. She put it on now and went down to show the family.

There was a general gasp of horror as she walked in, cackling like an old crone.

"Wow! Gruesome!" said Jimmy in admiration.

"It's perfect!" Francine exclaimed.

"Not quite," said her father. He left the room and came back with a handmade broom painted black.

"No witch is complete without her broom. So here you are, my dear," he said, handing the broom to Audrey with a deep bow.

"Oh, thanks, Daddy!" Audrey giggled with delight.

"And one thing more," said her mother. She came forward with, of all things, a big sequined bow, which she proceeded to thumbtack to the broom handle. Audrey stared in amazement, as the others burst into laughter.

"Mother, what are you *doing?* I can't spoil all this horror with something *pretty* like that!"

Mrs. Royal just smiled and patted her daughter's hand. "I can't send my awful witch out on Halloween without a little softening touch."

"But, *Mother* —"

"Now, Audrey, darling, you don't want to look like all the *other* witches on Halloween, do you?" She was looking very serious now, but Audrey knew she was joking.

"Well, all right, but I think it's plain silly."

Deep down, though, she had to admit it was

2

kind of nice. After all, how many witches did you see on Halloween with a chiffon-and-sequin bow on their broom handles? And this *was* her first party in Jupiter. . . .

"Look, we'd better get Jimmy ready," Francine said. "His friends will be here soon, and we've got all that makeup to put on." Jimmy was eight, and Francine, who was "twice as old as he was" liked to act the big sister.

This was the first year Francine wasn't doing anything special for Halloween and she seemed to be enjoying helping Jimmy and Audrey get ready for their night of fun. But Audrey knew her sister was making the best of things. It hadn't been easy for Francine to find friends since they had moved to Jupiter from New York, six weeks ago. It was Francine's first year in high school, where most of the boys and girls had known each other since kindergarten, and though they were all nice to Francine, she'd been feeling pretty much left out of things.

It had been different for Audrey and Jimmy. There were only two sixth-grade and two third-grade classes in their school, which was three blocks from their house, and many of the boys and girls lived nearby. So in a week's time they had so many friends they spent almost no time alone.

Audrey felt bad about Francine. But when

she said so to her mother one day before her sister got home from school, Mrs. Royal told her, "Don't worry — Francine will find her own friends in her own time. We don't all do things in the same way."

Audrey knew what her mother meant — Audrey had to have a whole circle of friends surrounding her or she felt absolutely lost. Francine was different. She liked to spend her free time on things that interested her, and she'd always had a few good friends to share her interests with. As for Jimmy, his single requirement was to have someone to play ball with or build models with, though, of course, that someone had to be a boy.

Now the doorbell rang. When her father opened the door, there was a chorus of "Trick or Treat!" Audrey peered into the hall and saw a bunch of third-grade boys with huge paper bags. Mrs. Royal handed out Halloween treats as she explained that Jimmy would be ready soon.

"Hurry up, Francine!" Audrey called, but just then Jimmy came bounding in; he wore a brightly patched shirt and baggy trousers, with a battered, torn hat tilted over one eye and charcoal smudged on his face. There were three other hobos in the group, all in similar garb. Jimmy yelled "Hi!" grabbed up his own bag, tied it to a stick that he slung over his shoulder, and ran out with his friends.

Just before the door closed, a trio of girls pushed inside, their giggles changing to shrieks of delight over Audrey's costume. Audrey introduced her new friends to her family: Patsy, a tall, thin girl in a bright gypsy outfit; Doris, a chunky, brown-blond ballerina, who never went anywhere without her new birthday wrist watch; and Joan, a lovely princess with silvery hair falling in a shimmering cloud from a lacy crown.

"Do you have your flashlight?" they asked Audrey as they were about to leave.

"Oh, I forgot!" She ran back to get one. "What's it for, anyway?" she asked.

Patsy shrugged. "I don't know — Lorraine wouldn't say, but she told each of us to bring one."

They waved a casual good-bye to the Royals and hurried outside.

A row of big trees half hid the streetlights; the bare boughs looked spooky against the moonlit sky. Huddling close, the girls shivered in the autumn chill as they rushed along toward Lorraine's house on the next block.

They rang Lorraine's bell, and, like magic, the door flew open and a bunch of hobos, clowns, and ghosts pushed out, whooping merrily as they ran down the steps.

"Hey, we saw that already — at Audrey's house!" Patsy cried, and the girls shrieked with laughter.

"Same scene — different characters," Doris said, setting off more laughter.

"Does this happen every place where there are little brothers?" Joan asked.

Audrey, still laughing, replied, "I guess you don't have a little brother or you'd know!"

"Girls, come on in — the party's all ready." Lorraine stood in the doorway looking almost like a twin to Audrey in her witch costume. But on seeing Audrey's broom with its fancy bow, she howled with delight. "Oh, how brilliant of you, Audrey. That's absolutely the neatest idea!"

Audrey had just opened her mouth to confess whose idea it had really been, when Lorraine's mother and father came to welcome and admire each girl, and then shoo them downstairs.

The basement was dimly lit, and as the girls made their way down carefully, they screamed at the sight of a skeleton dangling in midair, its bones glowing in fluorescent horror. Jack-o'-lanterns peered from two corners, some ghostly music was playing, and a table of goodies stood against a wall that was covered with black paper cats, bats, witches, and monsters.

The girls exclaimed over the decorations, to Lorraine's delight.

"Oh!" Patsy gazed longingly at the table. "My favorites — chocolate-covered doughnuts."

"Where?" Doris asked.

Lorraine hooted with laughter. "Blind as a bat! There, silly, right in front of your nose. Hey, let's get started with our games. My folks are making me share the party with Donald." She glanced at Audrey. "You know brothers! When Don and his gang get back from trick-or-treating, they're coming down here. They'll eat everything in sight."

Joan eyed the gallons of cider and the plates piled high with doughnuts. "I guess there'll be plenty for all of us," she said.

Doris smacked her lips. "Not after I get my teeth into them!"

"Anyway," Patsy said, "let's not take chances. What are we going to play first, Lorraine?"

"Let's start with Mr. Bones here," she replied, pointing to the skeleton. "Gee, Rosie and I planned all the games and things last week, and then she had to go and get sick! We'd have even more fun with her here."

"You bet we would," Patsy said, turning to Audrey. "Do you know Rosie?"

Audrey had a dim recollection of a very large girl, but it was hard to remember everyone she'd met. "I think I met her once."

"Don't worry, you'll get to know her soon enough," Doris promised. "She's *something*."

"She has bronchitis," Joan explained. "We thought she'd be better by Halloween, but the doctor said she still has to stay in."

Lorraine groaned. "I bet her mother'll have to lock her in tonight to keep her from coming here. Imagine Rosie Kramer having to stay home on *Halloween*! Look, kids, let's get going with the games now, okay?" She produced five black half-masks with pieces of cellophane tape on each side. "First is 'Pin the Mask on the Ghoul.' But instead of pinning, we're going to tape. Oh, the blindfold." She waved a black kerchief and beckoned to Doris to begin. They blindfolded her, turned her around three times, and gave her a shove toward the skeleton, and she let out a scream when she bumped into it — to everyone's delight.

After everyone had a turn, they stood looking at the skeleton with the black masks taped all over its bones. Joan had come closest to the eye sockets. She had taped the mask over its mouth, and was awarded a giant chocolate bar.

"Next is the big surprise," Lorraine announced. "We're going to have a scavenger hunt — outside!"

"Outside!"

"Oh, scary!"

"How can we find things in the dark?"

"So *that's* why we had to bring flashlights!"

"You'll each get a list of ten things to find, and a shopping bag to put them in," Lorraine explained. "You have your flashlights, and you're limited to my backyard and Doris's, two houses away. I checked with your mother," she told Doris. "Now, I can't play, of course, because I made up the lists — Rosie helped me. All the things are somewhere in my yard and Doris's and you have to find them. You'll have half an hour, and I'll float around and see that everything's okay."

Lorraine distributed the lists. The girls groaned, giggled, and exclaimed as they read off the items: a milk bottle, a gold button, a tennis ball, a green shoe, a penny, an argyle sock with a hole in the toe, a red flannel nightshirt, a comic book, a teddy bear, and a used lipstick.

They hurried out the back door and began their scramble for the treasures, their flashlights flickering in the dark yard.

The houses in this small Pennsylvania town

in "Dutch country" were attached for whole blocks. Set in neat rows, each had a long, narrow backyard, many with garages at the far end. These faced onto alleys that ran parallel with the streets, and the alleys served as playgrounds and meeting places for the young people.

Now the girls' activity sparked curiosity in all the surrounding houses. One light after another was switched on in upstairs rooms, and from the lighted windows faces peered down at the strange goings-on below. The party guests were too busy to pay attention to anything but their quest, and each time another treasure was unearthed — from strange places like under leaf piles, behind outdoor furniture, or among the shrubbery, there was a cry of triumph. Groans of disappointment greeted Lorraine's call of "Time!" But they all returned to her basement happily enough with their bags of treasure, hands cold and muddy, appetites sharpened by the night air.

Each girl made a pile of her finds, and Lorraine checked. Out of the ten items on the list, Audrey had found nine; the other girls had eight each.

"Wow, that was close," Lorraine said after the tally. "One more for all of you, and it would have been a four-way tie. And how can you split a piece of precious jewelry four ways?

Audrey tore away the wrappings and opened a small box. A rubber devil's head goggled crazily at her from atop a gold-colored ring. Everyone wanted to try it on, and the sight of their muddy fingernails set them laughing again.

"Okay," Lorraine said, "let's line up for the sink."

"And *then*," Doris declared, "we *eat*."

For a few minutes no one talked — only the sounds of munching and sipping could be heard. But by the time they'd reached thirds, they were busy reliving the scavenger hunt, going over the details. Suddenly there was a thunderous rumble at the basement door, and once again hobos, ghosts, and clowns swooped down, waving their Halloween bags triumphantly as they headed for the table of food.

Lorraine beckoned to the girls to watch as she opened up the boys' bags, silently admiring their booty of popcorn, cookies, apples, and candy bars. The boys were too busy talking and helping themselves to the cider and doughnuts even to notice, and the girls caught snatches of their conversation about their doorbell-ringing adventures.

"Remember when we were little and used to go around for trick-or-treat...?" Patsy began.

"One year I got enough goodies to last me two months!" Doris interrupted.

Then the girls found some dried corn left in the bottom of the boys' bags. As they ran it through their fingers, they explained to Audrey how, in the weeks before Halloween, the kids would go down to the cornfields and pick off all the old ears that had been left there. They'd bring them home, let them dry out, and then shuck off the kernels and put them in a paper bag for Halloween.

"We used to throw the kernels on porches and at windows," Patsy said to Audrey. "*You* know, if people didn't give us anything."

"Oh." Audrey suddenly remembered the time — she must have been six or seven — when it had occurred to her to wonder what the "trick" part of "trick-or-treat" meant. Her mother had laughingly explained that you were supposed to play a trick on people if they didn't give you a treat. But everyone in her town had always given things to the children who came on Halloween. "Does that ever happen?" Audrey asked now.

Patsy and Joan laughed, and Lorraine said, "Hey, why don't we go out and ring a few doorbells?" We won't be able to have any more fun here anyway, with the boys around. And we can take this corn — they've got loads left over. Let's show Audrey what it's like!"

They all jumped at the idea, secretly pleased at the chance of doing once again the things that had always been the most fun on Halloween.

Taking the dried corn for tricks, and the shopping bags for any treats, they decided to start at the Moyers' house down the street.

"Mrs. Moyer is the best baker in Jupiter," Joan told Audrey. "We always used to go to her house first on Halloween to be sure to get some cookies before they were all."

"All what?" Audrey asked.

"That's a Pennsylvania Dutch expression," Lorraine explained. "It means 'to get used up.'"

Mrs. Moyer had plenty of cookies left tonight, and she made a big fuss over the girls. "I've missed you since you all got so grown up. It's about time you came around. Don't forget to come back for my Christmas cookies."

"And your doughnuts on Fastnacht Day," Doris said. As they went down the steps later, Audrey asked, "What's Fastnacht Day?"

Her friends looked at her in amazement, and Patsy exclaimed, "Don't tell me there's no Fastnacht Day where you come from!"

"Of course not, silly!" Lorraine said. "It's a

Pennsylvania Dutch holiday. They don't celebrate it in New York." She turned to Audrey. "Fastnacht Day is Shrove Tuesday, the day before Ash Wednesday. Like Mardi Gras, in New Orleans. It's the start of the fasting before Easter, and here the Pennsylvania Dutch make these yummy doughnuts by frying them in deep fat, and they're just—well, you'll see when you taste them."

There it was again: Pennsylvania Dutch! Audrey's mother and father thought it was so charming and colorful. In fact, when they'd still lived in New York, and long before her father was transferred to Jupiter, Mr. and Mrs. Royal had taken a weekend trip to the Amish country — a little farther south in Pennsylvania — and had returned home all excited over the Pennsylvania Dutch customs they had learned about and seen. They explained to Audrey and Jimmy that "Dutch" really meant "German," from the word "Deutsch."

Audrey and her sister and her brother had been intrigued by their descriptions and with the little souvenirs they had brought home. So when the girls learned they would be moving to Jupiter, in the heart of the Pennsylvania Dutch country, they had looked forward to sharing all the quaint customs. But it was turning out to be much different from what Audrey expected. This unfamiliar place had not only its own holidays, its own art, and its own foods, but even its own language! Of course, it *was* interesting and quaint ... but Audrey just couldn't get used to constantly bumping up against customs and words she didn't know. Sometimes it seemed like living in a foreign country!

"Hey, girls," Lorraine said now, as they passed the next house, shrouded in darkness, "let's go to the Trexlers'." Audrey heard the suppressed excitement in her voice, and noticed that the other girls hung back as Lorraine advanced toward a rickety porch.

Audrey glanced from face to face. "What's wrong?" she asked. "Anyway, there aren't any lights on downstairs. Do you think we ought to be here?"

"I don't," answered Joan. "The Trexlers are real sourpusses. We *never* used to come here for trick-or-treat. Everyone was always scared of them, remember?"

"That's the point!" Lorraine cried. "We're bigger now — they can't scare us, can they? Remember how we always used to say that one day we'd go there on Halloween?"

"Yes," Patsy said, caught up with Lorraine's excitement, "and we never did!"

"Well, it's about time," Doris declared. "Anyway"— and she rattled the bag of corn — "what did we bring this along for?"

At that, Lorraine turned and ran up the Trexlers' steps, with Patsy and Doris following close behind. Joan stayed down close beside Audrey.

The three girls turned back to them from the shadows of the porch, and Lorraine whispered, "You don't have to if you're chicken!"

Joan edged closer against Audrey, who took a tentative step forward and then stopped as she heard thumping on the porch. But it was only the other girls running over to the door to ring the bell. Suddenly, a light flashed on in the vestibule, outlining the faces of the three girls, and just as suddenly it went off. Then the door squeaked open a crack, and the trio chanted, "Trick or treat!" As they held their bags hopefully open, there was a loud splash, a round of screams, and the shocked, dripping retreat of a soggy witch, a gypsy, and a ballerina.

"My *watch* got wet!" Doris screeched.

Audrey burst out laughing, then stopped. "I'm sorry — it just sounded so funny!"

"Listen," said Lorraine, the water dripping from her drooping witch hat, "we're going to absolutely *drown* their house in corn!" She dug vehemently into her bag. The others did the same, and they threw the dried corn as hard as they could at the windows.

"I hope we break them all!" Doris cried, close to tears.

"Me too, those old — old *goblins*," Patsy said, heaving another handful.

The corn hitting the windows and the porch floor sounded like a rain of stones, as Audrey joined in the slinging.

Suddenly, the vestibule light flashed on again, and as suddenly, the five girls turned and fled down the street. Patsy took the lead and they turned into her block, not stopping until they reached her front porch. "Why don't we all come into my house and get dried off?" Patsy asked.

Suddenly Lorraine let out a terrible howl. "My *bag* got wet!"

Doris and Patsy quickly checked their own, breathing sighs of relief at finding their treats dry and unharmed. Patsy invited them all inside and got towels for them.

"Listen," Lorraine said as they left Patsy's house, "let's get up early tomorrow morning and watch the Trexlers clean off their porch."

"We could offer to help — and then laugh," Doris said.

"You can if you want to," Joan told them, "but I'd rather not."

"I guess we really shouldn't have gone there," Audrey said, "but still, they did a terrible thing. Just because you rang their doorbell."

"Don't they do that in New York?" Lorraine asked. When Audrey shook her head, Lorraine said, "You know, New York sounds like a nice place — but awfully dull."

Audrey had never thought about it that way. New York hadn't really been dull, but it hadn't been exciting, either. It had been just a place to live and grow up in and have fun in, like any other city — like Jupiter. . . . Or was that true? She wondered now. There were so many strange things about Jupiter. It was only about a hundred miles from New York, but it might just as well be on another planet.

"Look," Doris said, stopping, "the Millers have their porch light on. Let's go up."

"I wonder if Hope is home," Joan said as they trooped up the cement steps to the freshly painted porch. She turned to Audrey, explaining, "They're real strict. And *clean*. Mrs. Miller *scrubs* her porch and steps and sidewalk every morning."

"Her sidewalk?" Audrey repeated. "Why, I never heard of —"

But the other girls were already on the porch, turning something on the door that looked like a large, metal winding key. As they turned, Audrey heard a bell ringing, and realized it was an old-fashioned, hand-cranked doorbell.

A light flashed on, and all the girls stepped back, but when the door opened and a girl their age stood there smiling, they surged forward, crowding around her with their open bags. Only Audrey hung back, staring.

In the first moment, she didn't recognize Hope Miller, and thought she was looking at a live doll. Hope was dressed as a Dutch girl, from her long, blonde pigtails flying out beneath a starched white cap, down to an authentic pair of wooden shoes. Two round, blue eyes smiled at everyone, and she fluttered excitedly among them, filling their bags with home-baked cookies. Audrey finally recognized her as a girl she had often seen at school, usually alone, always looking very serious, and dressed — as one of the kids had said — to look like somebody's grandmother. Audrey glanced through the doorway at what appeared to be a very strange-looking room beyond, but the light in it was too dim to make out any details.

"Here's one for you." Hope was offering Audrey a big cookie decorated with a witch.

Audrey stared at it, fascinated. "Thank you very much. Did — did you make these?"

Hope smiled. "Well, I helped my mother and grandmother. You're the new girl, aren't you?"

"Oh, yes — I'm Audrey Royal. And you're Hope Miller."

Hope's face turned pink, then scarlet, and she dropped her eyes. Audrey was puzzled. Was Hope awfully shy — or did she feel the girls must talk about her as "that odd Hope Miller"? As Audrey wondered about it, Lorraine began tugging at her sleeve, saying, "Come on, Audrey, we better leave if we want to get to any other places."

A chorus of hurried thanks echoed through the little hallway as the girls rushed outside. Audrey turned to look back at the golden-haired girl. The night's shadow almost obscured her face now, but her bright hair still shone in the dim light.

"Gosh," Doris shrieked, consulting her watch, "it's almost ten o'clock! I have to go home."

They parted in a flurry, assuring one another that this had been the best Halloween of their lives — "except for the Trexlers."

"And we'll think of something for them," Lorraine said mysteriously.

20

chapter 2

Audrey met Lorraine and Patsy on the way to school next morning, and the three went over all the details of their Halloween night — giggling and talking all at once. But Audrey felt a little uneasy when Lorraine announced: "Listen, everybody, I have the perfect plan for the Trexlers. We're not going to let them get away with last night, don't think!"

"Of course not," Patsy agreed. "And let's not give *them* a chance to forget, either!"

"Oh, why don't we just leave it alone?" Audrey said. "We had our fun, and there are always party poopers around. Let's think of something else to do."

"Party poopers! What's *that*?" Patsy wrinkled up her nose. "A special New York word?"

Audrey laughed. "Not that I know of. It's

21

people who — well, I guess you'd say spoil other people's fun."

"Hey, I think *you're* the party pooper then," Lorraine said. "We can't let people like the Trexlers think they can treat us that way and get away with it. I mean, do you really think they were right?"

"Of course not!" Audrey exclaimed. "But that doesn't mean ..." She was stopped by the frown on Lorraine's face. Audrey was, after all, the new girl. And Lorraine was more fun than anyone she'd met in Jupiter so far, and had a lot of influence. "Anyway," Audrey said, "let's hear the plan."

"What's this about plans? What are you kids cooking up?"

Audrey spun around to face a heavyset girl with an unexpectedly dimpled smile.

"Rosie!" Lorraine squealed, grabbing the girl's arm. "You're *better*. We missed you last night. Why did you have to go and get bronchitis on Halloween?"

"Did you ever miss the fun!" Patsy cried, grabbing her other arm.

"I know, I know," Rosie groaned. "Don't you think I heard every gory detail the minute it was over? First Doris called, then Joan, and I tried phoning you, Lorraine, but your line was busy."

"Probably because I was trying to get you, but then it was late and my mother wouldn't let me stay up any longer. I didn't know you'd be coming back to school today or I would've stopped for you."

"I think it was all just a plot to ground me for Halloween. And I had to go and miss the greatest party in history! But I hear there's a little unfinished business to take care of, anyway, so maybe I'm not too late after all."

"Well, we don't know," Patsy put in. "Audrey thinks — hey, do you and Audrey know each other?"

Rosie studied Audrey. "You're the new girl from New York, *say*."

Audrey smiled at the Pennsylvania Dutch expression. "I guess my fame has spread around Jupiter. But I've heard a lot about you too. Rosie Kramer — right?"

Rosie grinned proudly. "Troublemaker, first class." She slapped Audrey lightly on the shoulder. "We have a lot of fun here. You'll see. Now, what's this about plans? It's for the Trexlers, I hope."

Lorraine beamed. "Of course. And I'll bet you've got some good ideas."

"I sure do. Listen . . ."

Rosie's plan was about the same as Lorraine's: they would get a group together that day after school — meeting just inside the main school door — converge on the Trexlers' house, and let them have it with all the dried corn they could find. Rosie volunteered to go up and ring the doorbell first, and this time they'd be quick as lightning and escape before the Trexlers knew what had struck.

"I made it my business to pass their house this morning," Lorraine announced then, "and there wasn't a kernel in sight. They must have been out there cleaning up at the crack of dawn." Suddenly, unexpectedly, she linked her arm through Audrey's and said, "You'll come with us, won't you?"

"Okay." Afterward, Audrey wondered if she would have joined them if Lorraine hadn't asked her especially.

They buzzed about it the rest of the way to school, but after Audrey left them inside the main corridor, she had a sinking feeling.

As she approached her homeroom, she felt a light, birdlike tap on her shoulder, and turned to find Hope Miller smiling at her shyly.

"Hello, Audrey."

"Oh, Hope! Hi. Whose room are you in?"

"Miss Bauer's. You?"

"Mrs. Frantz."

"We're right across the hall from each other." The bell sounded then. "Oh, I'll see you

24

later!" Hope called as she hurried toward her homeroom. Audrey watched her for a moment, fascinated by the odd sight of the doll-like girl in a dress way too long and shoes that could have been from the last century. How could she bear to look so old-fashioned?

"Come on, you'll be late." Sandra Parker had come up and took Audrey's arm, leading her inside the classroom.

Audrey was feeling pleased at having made so many friends here in Jupiter so quickly; she smiled at Sandra as they took their seats across from each other.

For a fleeting moment, she wondered again about Hope — and the thought struck her that if Hope had been the new girl, instead of Audrey, she would probably have been snubbed immediately by the "popular" group of girls. Being different from the rest — or, or least, *looking* different — was what could make you or break you.

The afternoon classes flew by. But once school was over, Audrey gathered her books for homework, and sighed with relief as the heavy school door closed behind her.

On the steps, she shook her head to clear it and breathed in the crisp November air. She liked this town, this school. Already she felt she belonged. Most of the kids knew her by

25

now; they greeted her as they passed, and many of them stopped to chat. Then she saw Hope waving to her, and started down the steps toward her, glad to have company to walk home. But suddenly she was pushed from behind; she let out a startled yelp.

"Hey, where've you been? We've been looking all over for you! We were supposed to meet *inside*, remember?"

It was Rosie, her hands on her hips, with Lorraine, Doris, and Joan trailing her.

Audrey slapped her forehead. "Ooh-h, I forgot!"

Just then, Patsy came rushing up, but stopped short when she saw Audrey. "Hey, we've been looking everywhere for you! How did you get out so fast?"

Rosie glared at Audrey. "Trying to escape from our clutches?" She grabbed her arm menacingly, then burst out laughing, and Audrey laughed then too.

"Hey, Audrey, you and I have something in common — dimples!" The other girls giggled, and they all started home together.

Too late, Audrey remembered Hope. She looked at the spot where Hope had been standing, but she had gone.

"Okay, now listen," Rosie was saying. "This is the way we're going to do it. We're going home and get our Halloween masks and all the corn we can find; then we'll meet on Lorraine's porch at four o'clock. After we get through, I don't think the Trexlers will ever pour another drop of water on another kid as long as they live."

After it was over, everyone agreed with Rosie that the whole thing had gone off perfectly. Rosie and Lorraine had managed to spread the word to some of the boys, who had eagerly joined the girls in bombarding the Trexler house with showers of dried corn. There they were, about a dozen Halloween-masked kids, all chanting a parody of an old rhyme as they threw the corn:

Halloween is coming and the geese are
    getting fat!
Since you didn't put a penny in the old man's hat,
Here's a trick, say Trexlers —
Take that and that and that!

It would probably take the Trexlers a whole day — or even two — to clean up the mess, they decided, chortling with satisfaction.

There was only one hitch: the Trexlers reported them to Mr. Marshall, the school principal. He quickly found out the names of all the vandals and called them to his office the next afternoon.

He was furious, even after they told him what the Trexlers had done to them. "Two wrongs don't make a right," he thundered. After a severe scolding, he told them he was going to speak to their parents and leave punishments up to them. Then he turned to Audrey and said:

"As for you, young lady, you're new here, and I don't know how much you had to do with it. I'll give you the benefit of the doubt, with the thought that you may not have known what you were getting into. I can't excuse this kind of behavior in anyone, though, so I'm going to report you to your parents along with the rest. But I want to give you, privately, some friendly advice."

He nodded at the rest of the group to leave. Audrey's heart pounded harder as she faced Mr. Marshall alone. But he spoke to her in an almost fatherly way.

"None of these boys and girls is really bad, Audrey, but some of them tend to be — er, troublemakers." He smiled at her now, and she relaxed the hard fists in her lap as she tried to smile back. "I understand the difficulties of living in a new town, going to a new school — but you're a smart girl with a fine background. The advice I have for you is very simple: Be careful about the people you choose as friends.

I know it's nice to be popular, but don't get yourself tangled up with a bad group."

Audrey left his office trembling with a mixture of shame and indignation. She was ashamed of being part of something that she had known in her heart was wrong; she was embarrassed at having been caught at it; and she was indignant at Mr. Marshall's saying first that none of the boys and girls involved was "really bad," and then finishing up by advising her not to get herself tangled up with a "bad group."

Now she'd have to face her parents. She knew the others feared punishments in terms of their allowances or new clothes, or watching television, or playing ball. But Audrey had no idea how her parents would punish her because she'd never done anything like this before.

Once home, she shut herself up in her room till dinner time, miserable and frightened, trembling each time the phone rang — but it never was Mr. Marshall. Finally, right after her father got home from work, she poured out to him and her mother a full confession, bursting into tears as she told the whole story from beginning to end. And, as if on cue, no sooner did she finish than Mr. Marshall telephoned.

Audrey held her breath as she listened to

her father explain that Audrey had just told them the whole story. His feeling, he said, was that Audrey's own misery at knowing she had done something wrong seemed to be punishment enough. Mrs. Royal nodded agreement, and Mr. Royal promised to see that his daughter was not involved in any such incidents in the future.

Then he added, "The fact that the Trexlers also did a disgraceful thing by throwing water on these kids merely for ringing their doorbell leads me to feel that some apology is due *from* them as well as *to* them."

For a moment Audrey was afraid her parents would make her apologize to the Trexlers, but they didn't. And she found out the next day that many of the other parents also felt the Trexlers were in the wrong — especially the parents of the girls who'd been showered!

Most of the kids received severe warnings, though, and the parents of Rosie and the boys did punish them, saying that they hadn't been a part of the original group and had no business "butting in." Rosie had her allowance cut off for two weeks, but she shrugged it off as an old story. "I can borrow from you kids again, can't I?" she said, smiling as they nodded. "And when you hear about my newest plan, you won't refuse me *anything*!"

"Oh-oh, it sounds like trouble," Joan said.

Rosie shook her head vigorously. "No, not this time — honest. In fact, it's sort of a way to prove to everyone — especially Mr. Marshall and my mom and dad — that we can do special things, just our own group, without it being trouble."

"Well, how?" Doris asked. "What would we do? What's your plan?"

Rosie looked around at each girl slowly, then replied in a loud whisper, "A secret club! Just for the six of us."

"Hey! That's a great idea!" Patsy and Doris chorused.

" But what *for*?" Joan persisted. "What *kind* of a club?"

"And why would it be secret?" Audrey asked.

"And why just us?" Lorraine added.

Rosie held up both hands. "Wait — I'll explain. Now, we've got to show everyone that they were wrong about us — especially Mr. Marshall. Audrey's told us he warned her about being careful not to get tangled up with the wrong group. You know, that makes us sound like — like — "

"Criminals!" Lorraine supplied. "And we weren't doing any more than little kids do on Halloween. You'd think we were juvenile delinquents or something!"

"But — but what'll we *do* in this club?" Doris asked again.

"Well, we'll all have ideas. But I was thinking about games after school — you know, like basketball, or skating, or hikes, and fun projects, and parties — "

"Well, that sounds okay, but why just the six of us?" Lorraine asked once more.

"And why should it be a *secret* club?" Patsy demanded.

"Look, don't you see?" Rosie replied patiently. "It was the six of us who got into trouble and Mr. Marshall said those things about, well, about *five* of us, except that Audrey was really one of us too. Well, if we form a club and do a lot of things just for fun, ourselves — I don't mean anything bad — well, even so, the minute Mr. Marshall hears about it, he'll *think* it's something bad. So will everyone else, for that matter. So we've got to keep it a secret for a while at least — our own parents would be suspicious after all this business. But if we have a club and do just good fun things, people won't be suspicious of us anymore. And then it won't have to be secret. And meanwhile, we can have a lot of fun together, just the six of us."

"It does sound like fun," Lorraine agreed. "And a secret club — boy, that's great! We could have secret meeting places, and dues, and everything."

Audrey looked at Rosie with a new feeling of warmth. She had been a little fearful of what this "troublemaker" might propose, ever since the corn-throwing. But now Rosie seemed only to want to prove to everyone that they were really okay. The other girls were excited about the club idea, and Audrey added her enthusiasm. "We could call it The Secret Six," she suggested.

"Oh, that's terrific!" Lorraine cried.

"Yes, yes — you're a genius, Audrey," Rosie added, slapping her shoulder with approval.

Suddenly everyone was talking at once, coming up with ideas and suggestions. They decided that the first meeting would be held the next day after school in Patsy's garage, when they would make more plans.

"And don't forget," Rosie warned as they were ready to part, "you *must* keep it a secret. The Secret Six must be the only ones in the *whole wide world* to know about the club!"

"Let's cross arms and link hands to seal the promise, all six of us," Lorraine said. And they did.

chapter 3

Audrey was ready to explode with her secret by the time she got home. Luckily her mother was on the telephone, so Audrey didn't break her promise. Maybe, she figured, the longer she avoided any talk, the easier it would be to keep the secret.

As she passed Francine's room, she heard voices behind the closed door. Since they'd moved here, Francine had never invited anyone to the house. So Audrey was overcome with curiosity, and knocked.

"Who is it?" her sister called.

"Mary Poppins," Audrey squeaked.

She heard laughter as the door opened and Francine grinned at Audrey. "Okay, then, where's your umbrella?" But Audrey's eyes were glued to the strangely made-up face that beamed at her from beneath a weird hairdo. Francine, the pretty, tawny-haired teenager, had darkened her eyes with makeup and piled her hair on top of her head.

"Hey," Audrey said, stepping inside and peering all around, "I thought Halloween was ov —" She stopped as she saw a lovely, elfin-looking girl half-lying on Francine's bed.

"Hi, I'm Sylvia Goldberg," the girl said. She had on the same eye makeup, but her dark, shiny hair curled in a soft roll on her shoulders.

"This is my sister, Mary Poppins," Francine said. Then she told Audrey, "Sylvia and I are in the same class in French and chemistry and history!" Her face was aglow now, not just her eyes, and Audrey realized she hadn't seen her look so happy since they'd moved here.

"Nice to meet you, Mary. I always wished I had a little sister instead of two bratty little brothers," Sylvia said.

Audrey giggled. "My name is really Audrey, and we've got one of those too."

"What?"

"Bratty little brothers. But just one."

"And *you*," Francine said, smiling sweetly at Audrey.

Audrey sniffed. "You don't mean I'm like *him!*"

"Oh, no — how could anyone even *think* such a thing!" But though Francine was laughing, Audrey felt a little hurt at her sister's sarcasm.

"Any time you don't want her, I'll take her," Sylvia said, winking at Audrey, and Audrey instantly liked her. Francine might take a while to make friends, but when she did, she certainly chose them well!

There was a sudden rumble on the stairs, and in the next moment three smudge-faced boys stood in the doorway. "Francine, Audrey — where's my model stuff?" screamed the dirtiest one of all.

Francine's eyes rolled toward the ceiling as she groaned, "Oh-h-h, here we go again!"

Audrey yelled back, "Jimmy Royal, how in the world would *we* know where your 'model stuff' is? Do you think *we* go around playing with it?"

Francine laughed. "I don't even know what 'model stuff' you mean."

"Aw, you do so! And you prob'ly hid it. I looked all over, and — " His eyes lit on Sylvia. He stared, then asked, "Who's *she?*"

Francine addressed Sylvia with ultra-politeness. "Sylvia, this is my well-mannered little brother, James, and his friends, Wimp and Clifford. Boys, this is Sylvia Goldberg."

"Hiya, James," Sylvia said.

"Hiya. My name isn't James. It's Jimmy. *What's* yours? Silver-and-Gold-Berg?" He guffawed at his cleverness, and his friends laughed loudly and shoved at each other. Francine, reddening, said, "Very funny. Now look, *James,* go find your model stuff — whatever and wherever it is — and leave us alone. Go put on your comedy act somewhere else!" She pushed them toward the door and closed it firmly behind them. "Ugh!" she exclaimed, "why couldn't we have a nice, handsome *big* brother instead — one with lots of gorgeous friends!"

Audrey, perched on the edge of the bed beside Sylvia, felt flattered at being included as one of the older girls. "What were you two putting on that stuff for?" she asked.

She was just starting to lean back, when Francine took her hand and gently pulled her to her feet, saying, "Oh, we've been fixing our hair and things. You wouldn't be interested, so we'll be happy to excuse you." She pointed her toward the door, and Audrey, crushed, turned back toward Sylvia. "It was nice to meet you, Sylvia, and I hope you come again." With a sidelong glance at Francine, she continued, "And thank you for those nice compliments you gave me before. I'd take *you* for a big sister any time." Glaring at Francine openly now, she cried, "I have *my* secrets too, and won't *you* be surprised when you find out! But you never will."

With that, she tossed her head and pranced out of the door and into her own room, slamming the door and collapsing on her bed in misery. Here she was, with the most marvelous secret in the world, and she couldn't share it. She'd have to wait a whole day to talk about it again, unless she phoned one of the girls. ... Her thoughts were suddenly interrupted by the sight of an unfamiliar pile of boxes stacked high on her desk. "Jimmy's model stuff!" she said aloud. Pouncing on it, she discovered seven boxes of his paraphernalia bound together with twine. She grabbed it and flew downstairs, almost colliding with her mother in the kitchen.

"Oh, Audrey, where in the world did you find *those?* Jimmy's been raising the roof and accusing everyone of hiding them or throwing them out."

"Well, I guess he was right, because they were hidden on *my* desk, and I can assure you I never — "

"Oh-h-h, that's right!" Mrs. Royal tapped her forehead in sudden recollection. "I found some twine in your desk, and I'd just finished tying them together to take back to his room, when the doorbell rang. I must have dropped them on your desk to run downstairs — and then forgot all about them." She gave Audrey a conspiratorial smile. "He'll have a fit when he finds out!"

They laughed over it while Mrs. Royal fixed them a snack. Audrey was dying to tell her mother about the Secret Six, but she remembered her solemn promise not to breathe a word of it to anyone, so instead told her about Hope and how they had missed out on getting to know each other.

"Well, then, why don't you just pick up the phone and invite her over?" Mrs. Royal suggested. "It seems to me she'd be delighted with an invitation, especially since she's made all the attempts at friendship so far."

"Yes, that's true. And she seems so nice."

Mrs. Royal just smiled and pointed to the telephone.

Audrey was glad she'd taken her mother's advice, because Hope sounded really happy to hear from her. "Oh, thank you, Audrey, that would be very nice, but — well, I'll come to your house next time. Would you want to come here first?"

Something stopped Audrey from asking why; instead, she said, "Just a minute, I'll ask my mother." At her mother's nod, she added, "It's okay."

All the way to Hope's house Audrey wondered why Hope had reversed the invitation, and decided that she would simply ask her at the first opportunity.

She remembered on Halloween night one of the girls describing Hope's house as "the one with the yellow-and-black banisters." That made it easy to recognize. On Halloween, of course, it had looked like the one on either side of it. All row houses in Jupiter seemed to be built alike.

Audrey also remembered her friends telling her that Hope's mother actually scrubbed her front steps and sidewalk every morning. It must be true, she thought now, and, almost gingerly, she hurried up the porch steps, hoping she wouldn't leave marks. She examined the carved metal key as she twisted it to ring the bell, and was startled when the door opened almost immediately.

"Hello!" Hope, looking pleased, shyly gestured for her to come in. Though the sun was still shining, the light didn't penetrate the tiny vestibule. And as Hope opened the inner door, leading to the living room, Audrey had to blink several times to accustom her eyes to the dimness. In the soft light of a small table lamp the room gradually came into focus.

Audrey had never seen a room like this before. Ranged about were huge pieces of furniture with dark upholstery and carved wood framework. A number of small tables were placed about the room, all covered with fringed cloths in deep colors, and the walls were crowded with various cabinets and rows of pictures. Suddenly, she noticed a dark figure seated in the chair beside the lamp.

"Audrey, I want you to meet my grandmother, Mrs. Heinz." Hope led her to the chair, and now Audrey saw more clearly a woman all in black, her skirts down almost to the tops of high laced shoes — the kind Audrey had seen in pictures of her great-grandparents. The woman, square-faced and with iron-gray hair combed straight back, looked stern. But the smile she gave Audrey was surprisingly warm.

"How — how do you do, Mrs. Heinz?" Audrey faltered, trying for her brightest smile.

"How do," replied Mrs. Heinz with a brief nod, still smiling but looking Audrey over very carefully. She turned to Hope and said something in another language that Audrey could recognize by now as Pennsylvania Dutch. Hope replied in the same language, and then, grasping Audrey's hand, said, "Would you like to go up to my room?"

Audrey nodded, then turned back to Mrs. Heinz to say, "It was nice to meet you." The woman nodded and smiled again, but Audrey was relieved to follow Hope up a steep, dimly lit staircase that led from the living room to the second floor. On the way, she glimpsed the dining room just beyond. It was too dark to see very much, but she did notice a large table spread with a gleaming white cloth and all the places set for dinner, even though it was only a little after four o'clock.

"My mother will be home soon," Hope explained as she led Audrey into the first bedroom off the hall. "She's at the store."

A little china lamp with a ruffled shade cast a soft light in the small room, and Audrey's eyes were drawn to the four-poster bed in the corner. It was covered with a patchwork quilt that was the brightest object she had seen so far.

"My grandmother made it," Hope said proudly, as Audrey examined the squares of cloth, all in different colors and designs. She

42

glanced at the dark wood dresser opposite, with its bellied front and elaborately carved legs. The top was decorated with small china figurines of children, animals, and ladies in beautiful old-fashioned gowns. "Does your mother collect antiques?" Hope asked, as she watched Audrey looking at her display. Audrey shook her head. "No, not really, but she has some things from her mother and grandmother, and she loves them. You know things like dishes and vases and stuff — but not very many."

Hope nodded, unsmiling. "Oh, yes, I know. Our house is all full of them. My mother and grandmother love them too."

"Do they collect them?"

"No, they just — *have* them."

"Oh. I have two friends back in New York and their mothers are real antique bugs. They go around to all the shops and to auctions, looking for treasures. They have beautiful display cabinets, and they'd just drool when they came to our house and saw anything older than five years! Boy, they would go *wild* here!"

Hope giggled. "I guess they would!"

Audrey's eyes moved on to the other side of the room. In a corner alcove stood a large, square desk, piled with Hope's schoolbooks and papers. Beside it was an enormous wooden cabinet with all kinds of doors and drawers. As if reading her mind, Hope went over to it. She switched on a desk lamp that cast a good bright light.

"This is where I keep all my things." Hope explained, opening the various doors and drawers, and Audrey saw games, craft sets, sewing supplies, and all sizes and shapes of boxes.

Hope took off the covers of the boxes to show Audrey what she had. There were all kinds of colored beads, ribbons of satin and velvet, and scraps of material. Hope had a collection of shells and stones, and there was one box full of all kinds of things — from magnets to marbles. When Audrey noticed a white linen handkerchief with a blue crocheted edging, she exclaimed, "Oh, how lovely! Did your mother make this?" She fingered the pretty petal-shaped border.

Hope smiled and her eyes sparkled. "No, I did."

"*You* did? Really?"

"Of course. Don't you know how to crochet? It's the easiest thing in the world. My grandmother taught me a couple of years ago when I had the mumps."

"*That's* why I can't crochet," Audrey declared. "One of my grandmothers lives in California and the other in Canada — I don't even know if they can crochet — and I never had the mumps."

"I hope you never do," Hope laughed. "But crocheting's fun to do sometimes, and you can make the nicest presents. Would you like me to show you how?"

"I'd love it! Would you really?"

"Of course." Hope poked around in a box that held pieces of material, and finally held up a white square of cloth. "This would be perfect. Would you like to make an edging for this?" She then found several colors of crochet thread and after Audrey chose a bright pink, Hope patiently taught her the basic crochet stitch and helped her until she was able to do it quite well herself. "We'll make the edging separately this time and sew it on later. I'll do a piece for another side," Hope said after Audrey was well under way, "and we can work together."

In a little while, Audrey felt as though she had always known Hope. Somehow, concentrating on their work, they slid into an easy conversation. Audrey found out that Hope was an only child, that her father worked in a local bank, and that her grandmother on her mother's side had come to live here after her husband died — before Hope was born. Her father's parents lived in Ohio and they took a trip there every summer, which was the high point of Hope's vacation because there were many cousins living there also, and several were her age.

Hope asked Audrey many questions about her family and about New York and her friends there, but she never mentioned her own friends. Audrey wondered, but she didn't want to ask because she was afraid of the answer. In thinking back, she realized she'd never seen Hope with anyone. Even on Halloween night, she had been home alone instead of at one of the many parties or even with just one other friend.

"Look," Hope suddenly exclaimed, "you're finished!"

And sure enough, Audrey had completed her part of the border. "Oh, it's *pretty*, isn't it?" she said, thrilled with her handiwork. Hope had completed hers too, and when they placed the border around the handkerchief, Audrey beamed with pride.

"Here, let me sew it on," Hope offered. "Then you'll have a nice souvenir to take home."

"Take home? You mean to — to show my mother?"

Hope shrugged. "Whatever you want. It's yours — you can do what you want with it."

"Mine? You mean to *keep?*"

"Of course."

"Oh, Hope, *thank* you."

Hope blushed a little. "I had a good time. I like to teach. And besides, these things are always more fun to do with someone."

There were noises downstairs that Audrey hadn't noticed before, and then a sharp call: "Hope, it's after five o'clock!"

"Mama! I didn't even know you were home yet." Hope turned to Audrey. "I have to stop now. We — we eat supper early."

They quickly put away the crochet materials and Audrey said, "I still have my homework to do, so I really should be leaving now, anyway."

Mrs. Miller was waiting at the bottom of the steps, and Hope introduced her friend.

"How do." Mrs. Miller greeted Audrey with a warm smile. "Come again, *say now.*" Audrey knew this Pennsylvania Dutch expression was tacked onto many sentences; in this case it meant, "Won't you?"

She replied politely, "I will, thank you. And I'd like Hope to come visit me too." She turned to her new friend and said, "Will you — soon?"

Hope glanced at her mother; then, nodding eagerly, replied, "Oh, yes, Audrey, I'd love to!"

Audrey realized as she walked home that she

had had to be approved by Hope's mother —
and probably her grandmother — and that was
probably the reason why Hope wouldn't come
to the Royals' house first. Now that she had
been "passed on and approved," their friendship was officially "allowed" by Hope's mother
and grandmother.

Anyway, she told herself, Hope was really
nice, and fun. In fact, the time she'd spent with
Hope had been one of the most pleasant she'd
had since they'd moved to Jupiter.

chapter 4

The meeting had been called for four o'clock in Patsy's garage, but by a quarter to four everyone was there. It was a very tidy place, with a narrow bench lining one wall and a miniature worktable in a corner. Two small windows were hung with plastic café curtains which Rosie carefully drew, explaining, "This really makes it private."

"Nobody even knows we're here," Patsy said, as they compared the excuses they'd made to come.

"It's secret for sure!" Joan cried. Then she added, "What about your brothers, Patsy?"

"Paul has Scouts and Kenny is over at my uncle's. It all worked out just right."

"Look," Doris said, pulling a jar out of her coat pocket. "My mother made it this morning. Can you get some bread or crackers or something, Patsy?"

"What is it?" Audrey asked, eyeing the dark-brown contents.

"Apple butter. I couldn't ask to take it because then my mother would have wanted to know why. But she won't even notice just one jar missing — she made a huge batch."

Then Rosie dug into her own coat pocket, saying, "Look what *I* have!" Triumphantly, she produced a big bag of peanuts.

"A party!" they all cried. Patsy hurried to the house and returned with half a loaf of bread, a box of crackers, two knives, and some paper towels, which she laid on the worktable. They busily spread bread and crackers with the apple butter, and ate these between mouthfuls of peanuts.

Suddenly Lorraine let out a gasp. "Girls, it's a quarter after four, and we haven't discussed a single thing about the Secret Six yet!"

"Well," Rosie declared, "I think the first thing we ought to do it take an oath to *keep* it the Secret Six."

"What do you mean?" Joan asked. "The secret part, or the six part?"

Everyone laughed, but Rosie replied very seriously, "Both."

Audrey looked around at her friends, sitting here cozily at their secret club meeting, and thought about Hope, who was most likely at home in her bedroom, studying or doing needlework by herself. "I understand the secret part," she said, "but why only six? Suppose there's another girl we all like who might want to join?"

"Like who?" Lorraine said. "Hope Miller, maybe?"

At first, Audrey believed she meant it; but at the way everyone laughed, she realized with a shock that they thought Lorraine's remark a big joke. It wasn't sheer coincidence that Lorraine had used Hope as an example — obviously she was about the last person they would consider. As far as Audrey knew, none of them was aware that she had seen Hope outside of school yesterday. She felt her cheeks getting hot and was starting to say something in Hope's defense, when Rosie declared, "I think we ought to stick to just ourselves for now — we're the only girls who were involved in the big Halloween Massacre. That gives us a deep bond. Didn't we agree on six when we thought up the idea in the first place?"

At everyone's nod, Audrey realized she would probably do Hope more harm than good if she were to push for her now. But she was determined to fix it so that one day they would *beg* Hope to join the club. And if they didn't, she told herself, she would quit.

Now they began discussing how often they would have meetings.

"Well, we'd never manage to keep the club a secret if we met as often as once a week," Lorraine said.

"That's true," Patsy agreed.

"If we met only once a month," Audrey suggested, "we'd have something to look forward to the whole month."

"But how will we ever get anything done?" Joan asked.

Rosie shrugged. "It doesn't mean we can't do things in between, does it?"

"And we can keep working on whatever projects we're doing too," Patsy added.

They decided to take their first vote, and the result was to have regular meetings on the first Wednesday of every month. Now came the big question — what should the Secret Six do? — and everyone began talking at once. Finally, they settled on the best ideas: give a play, go roller skating, have a Saturday-afternoon movie party, make a scrapbook for the children's ward of the hospital, organize an after-school nursery play group, start a ball team, an arts-and-crafts project, having a learning-to-dance party, give a pet show, start a gardening service. . . .

"Why don't we vote on all these?" Lorraine suggested.

"Before we vote," Audrey put in, "maybe we should decide what *kind* of thing we want to do. You know, parties and other fun things, or doing some service for other people."

"How about both?"

"Yes, one of each, to start with!"

Everyone liked that, and they voted to start with the hospital scrapbook as their first service activity and the learning-to-dance party as their first fun project.

"But who will teach us?"

"Where can we have it?"

"And when?"

"In December, before Christmas," Rosie said. "We can plan it all at our next meeting."

When everyone agreed that was a good idea, Audrey offered, "We could have it at my house. We have a playroom in the basement that's perfect for dancing. My parents play bridge every Friday night, and we could pick a Friday they play at someone else's house. My sister knows all the latest dance steps, and I think her girl friend does too. I'm sure they'd be willing to teach us."

"But we'd have to remember to keep our secret — about being a club and everything."

"Oh, that wouldn't be hard. We could just make it look as though we all came over to visit Audrey one Friday after supper."

"Who's your sister's friend?"

"Sylvia Goldberg."

There was a sudden silence. Audrey looked around from one to the other of the girls. "Is something wrong?"

"Are — are *you* Jewish?" Doris stammered.

"Me? No. Why?"

When Doris just shrugged, Audrey added, "Are you?" All the girls burst out laughing, and Audrey felt herself blushing. "I wish someone would tell me what's so funny."

Lorraine looked a little embarrassed as she replied, "I'm sorry, Audrey, but I guess that, coming from New York, and all, you feel — different — about some things. Maybe you can't imagine what a funny idea it is to think that Doris or any of us might be Jewish!"

Audrey, a strange feeling growing inside her, said, "Funny idea? *Why?* Anyone could be. . . . If you want to go by names — Hoffman,

Hertz, Kramer —" She looked around at the girls who had those names. "Why, in New York I knew Jewish people with those same names."

"Oh, but we're not Jewish, Audrey — honest!" Patsy cried. "I guess it's because Pennsylvania Dutch names are German, and Jews often have German names too."

"Gee," Doris said, "I never thought of that."

"But Sylvia Goldberg is Jewish. There's no question of that," Rosie said. "That's one name you'll never find anyone has but a Jew."

Audrey squeezed her eyes shut for a moment. She had always had many different kinds of friends, including Jewish ones, but she had never heard this sort of discussion before.

"I still don't understand," Audrey said. "What difference does it make if someone's Jewish? Supposing I were? Would it matter?"

The exchange of looks startled her. But Lorraine replied, "Of course not, Audrey. We —" She shrugged. "Well, I guess we're just not used to having Jews for friends. You know. They stick together and all. Leastways, here in Jupiter they do. But we don't have anything against them, do we?"

They shook their heads so vigorously, Audrey relaxed. She felt they were sincere, and thought maybe she had jumped to conclusions too fast. What Lorraine said was true: the

55

Jewish kids she'd seen at school did tend to stick together.

"Hey, it's five o'clock," Joan announced. "I have to go home!" They hurriedly decided to plan the details of their activities as soon as they could all get together again, but before the next regular meeting.

Audrey almost fell over Jimmy near their front steps. She hadn't noticed him, lying low in a game of cowboys with Wimp and Clifford, who were holding the fort on the front porch. She closed the door gratefully behind her to shut out their noise.

There were no lights on downstairs, and the living room was so dim as she passed through it that a sudden movement on the sofa terrified her. She quickly switched on a lamp and saw two little boys huddled together. They seemed about Jimmy's age, but she couldn't remember ever having seen them before. "Who are you?" she asked.

"Steven Goldberg," one boy replied, his lip trembling slightly. "This is my brother, Bobby."

"Oh-h, you must be Sylvia's brothers!"

They nodded soberly, and Audrey now saw that Bobby had tear streaks on his face.

"What's wrong?" she asked. "Why are you kids here all alone? Did Sylvia bring you?"

They both nodded. Then Steven, still the spokesman, said, "She and Francine went to the store. They told us to stay here till they came back. Who are you?"

Audrey laughed. "I'm Audrey, Francine's sister. But why did they leave you here all alone? Why aren't you playing with Jimmy and his friends?"

Steven bit his lower lip, and Bobby blurted, "We don't want to play with them! They made fun of us."

"They called us names, and they teased," Steven went on. "So, we're waiting here till Sylvia comes back. She has the key to our house — our mother isn't home."

"Well — well ... I wonder where *my* mother is?"

When both boys just shrugged, Audrey decided to look for her. But just then, Sylvia and Francine came in, carrying packages.

"Hey, why aren't you kids outside with Jimmy and his pals?" Francine asked the boys.

At that, Bobby burst out crying, ran to his sister, and buried his face in her skirt. After Steven explained, Audrey asked her sister, "Where's Mother?"

Francine said, "She's up in the attic unpacking some things. At least, she *was* when I got home from school. She probably can't hear us from up there." She turned toward the door, saying, "Wait till I get hold of Jimmy —"

Sylvia reached out and stopped her. "No, please, Fran, wait till we're gone. Here, boys, get your jackets. It's time to go home now, anyway."

"I'm awfully sorry," Fancine told her as they were leaving.

Just as the sisters started upstairs to find their mother, Mrs. Royal came down. Before she could say a word, Audrey burst out with some of the story, hardly stopping for breath.

"Well, how — why — what?" her mother finally managed.

Francine explained: "After you went up to the attic, Sylvia came over with her little brothers. She was supposed to take care of them while her mother went to the dentist, so I told her to bring them over here and they could play with Jimmy. One is the same age, and the other's a year younger, and I thought they'd have a good time together. Sylvia and I went over to the drugstore for some magazines and hair spray, and the boys were playing in the back yard when we left. My gosh, they looked happy enough! Wimp and Clifford were there too. They decided to play some kind of game, and we didn't think there was anything wrong. . . . And then, when we came back —"

"How long were you gone?" her mother asked.

Francine shrugged. "I don't know. We met some kids on the way back, and stopped to talk. I guess it was longer than we thought."

Mrs. Royal sat down on the sofa and the girls sat on either side of her.

"What shall we do?" Audrey asked.

"Wring Jimmy's neck!" Francine replied. "And give those two angelic little friends of his a piece of our minds too! Oh, Mom, I feel so bad for Sylvia — she was so hurt."

"You should have seen those little kids when I came in," Audrey said. "They were sitting here huddled against each other in the dark — probably bawling when they thought they were left alone."

"And I didn't hear a thing!" Mrs. Royal said. "I should have been here. I was rummaging around in the attic, and I really lost track of time."

"Hello, what's this? A Secret Female Society?" Mr. Royal had come in so quietly they hadn't heard him. Audrey thought: *If you only knew about a secret female society,* as they all reached for him at once. He landed in a laughing heap in a chair, muttering, "What a beautiful way to be massacred!"

"I didn't realize it was *this* late," Mrs. Royal began, but Francine interrupted, "Dad, something awful happened."

He sat bolt upright. "What?"

Mrs. Royal patted his shoulder. "Don't be alarmed — everything's really all right, dear. But we had an unfortunate experience between Jimmy and Sylvia's little brothers." She explained and her husband listened, frowning.

When she finished, he said, "I think we ought to start setting things straight around here. Jimmy's pals were still out there with him when I came in. Audrey, call Jimmy in — tell him it's time for dinner and for his friends to go home."

Now it was Jimmy's turn to tell what happened. The three of them had wanted to play cowboys, he said, but the Goldberg boys didn't want to play. So Wimp and Clifford said something like, "That's because Jewish kids don't know how to fight, anyway." The other two started crying and Wimp and Clifford began calling them "crybabies" and saying, "Why don't you go in the house and do crossword puzzles?"

60

"And what did you do, Jimmy?" Mr. Royal asked.

He shrugged, dropping his glance. "I don't know."

Francine sucked in her breath, then said, "What do you mean, you don't know..." But her father interposed.

"You must have done — or said — something, Jimmy. Now, think hard."

Jimmy's face turned scarlet. "Well, I *sort* of told Wimp and Clifford to leave them alone, and I told Steven and Bobby they could play with us if they wanted to."

"You did?"

"We-ell, I said if they stopped acting like babies and stuff, they could play with us, and otherwise to go in the house and watch TV or something till their sister came back."

"Oh, Jimmy!" said Audrey.

"Jimmy, remember Danny Friedberg in New York?" asked his father. "Remember how some kids picked on him about being Jewish, and you and your buddies put them down in a hurry?"

Jimmy looked up at his father now. "That was different, Dad! They were wrong — Danny was okay! It didn't have anything to do with being Jewish! Why, Danny was one of my best friends!"

"Then what makes these Goldberg boys different? Because they felt strange and Wimp and Clifford were mean to them? You let yourself go right along with your pals. That makes you as guilty as they are. Their words might just as well have come out of *your* mouth."

Jimmy stared at his father in disbelief. "But I never said anything like that! Who ever cared if anyone was Jewish or any old thing? *Boy*!"

"But don't you see," Mrs. Royal pointed out now, "by siding with Wimp and Clifford and letting them say those things at your house, it was just as bad as if you'd said them yourself?"

Listening, Audrey remembered the conversation about Sylvia at the Secret Six meeting earlier this afternoon. She suddenly saw that she herself had done almost what Jimmy had done — she'd simply accepted the remarks of her friends. True, she had started to argue with them, but then dropped it when they told her that was the way it was in Jupiter. She had told herself that some of their statements were true, like the one about the Jewish kids sticking together. Now she wondered if it wasn't because they were forced to.

"Well, I can't see why, just because my friends said something, it was as bad as if I said it!" Jimmy insisted. "I sure didn't mean it! I guess those Goldberg kids are sissies, but not because they're Jewish."

"And they're not sissies, either!" Francine cried. "They're just little boys who didn't know you and your friends and were never at our house before. Just because they didn't feel like doing what you wanted, does that make them sissies? How would you have felt if you were one of them?"

Jimmy started blinking very hard. He clenched his fists. "I don't know why everyone's picking on *me* . . ."

"Because you're responsible for something that happened at our home that we can't allow," Mr. Royal replied sternly. "Your mother and I have brought you children up to value human beings for themselves, and not judge them by the labels other people attach to them, like being Jewish or Catholic or white or black or rich or poor or —" He paused.

"Atheist?" Jimmy said, and Francine and Audrey couldn't help laughing. "That too," replied their father. "Every person is entitled to his own beliefs, just as everyone is entitled to a free choice in friends." He looked around at each of his children and added, "Mother and I feel very strongly about this, and we always assumed that you understood and felt the same way. It was easier in New York, of course. Some people here don't see things the way we do. And it comes as a shock to find that one of us has gone along with their narrow thinking."

Audrey squirmed in her chair. Had she too let her parents down this afternoon? And then there was the business of Hope. She'd taken the easy way out by remaining silent after they'd ridiculed Hope, instead of standing up for her.

"In any case," Mr. Royal concluded, "I hope that you've all learned a good lesson."

"What about Wimp and Clifford?" Jimmy asked.

Mr. Royal shrugged. "They're not my children. But they're your friends, Jimmy, and if they respect you, they'll respect your ideas. It's up to *you* to try to show them where they're wrong."

Jimmy grimaced. "Why do things have to get *so complicated?* It never was like this back in New York. We had *fun* back there. Why did we have to move here in the first place?"

Francine put her face into her cupped palms. "Why, indeed? This really is a square town!"

"It sure is! Audrey chimed in. "Everybody's got such crazy ways of doing things and looking at things ..."

"And I sure miss my friends back home," Jimmy said.

"Me too," said both the sisters at once.

"Hey, remember when you brought home those kids from the play center, Dad, and we camped out in our back yard?"

"And the time our whole block rented a horse and wagon and went on a hayride?"

"And the kids gave a circus and trained their pets to do tricks and we gave the money to the Community Chest . . ."

Soon Mr. and Mrs. Royal were reminiscing too, and as they grew more and more enthusiastic about the good times they'd had in New York, the children grew quieter and more and more thoughtful. Audrey finally burst out, "Oh, I wish we could go back to live there and be with all our old friends again!"

"So do I!" said Francine.

Their parents suddenly stopped smiling. "But, my dears," Mrs. Royal said, "you know we can't! Dad has been transferred here, and it's where we have to live — for the time being. Besides, it's really a lovely town. I know it's hard to make new friends and meet new attitudes, head on. But it's really just a matter of time, believe me. You've got all the people at school to choose from, and you'll get to know a whole new set of nice friends."

She paused, seeing the frowns on their faces.

"Oh, I know it isn't easy," she said. "But after the new, hard period is over, you'll see, it'll be just the same as it was back home. People are really pretty much the same everywhere. You'll always find some you like better than others."

"And," Mr. Royal added, "before you give up on Jupiter, just remember that you've only been here six short weeks. Now, stop and think of how many friends you've made already."

"And how much trouble we've gotten into already!" Jimmy piped up.

At that, everyone laughed and Mr. Royal said, "I suppose that trouble is part of what makes living interesting. Now how about some dinner?"

chapter 5

The next week, Hope came to Audrey's house one day after school. It was a really pleasant afternoon. The girls didn't do anything special — just talked and looked at Audrey's things. Hope looked through Audrey's autograph book and photo album from New York and asked many questions about her friends and her life there. She seemed much more at ease with Audrey's family than Audrey would have expected.

When it was time for her to go and Mrs. Royal said, "Please come again soon," Hope's eyes lit up as she replied, "Oh, thank you, I'd love to! I had a wonderful time!"

"She's a darling girl," Mrs. Royal told Audrey afterward. "I hope you'll bring her around a lot."

"Mother," Audrey said, examining her fingernails, "none of the other kids ever bother with her. Do you — do you think it's just because she always wears those old-fashioned clothes her grandmother makes for her?"

Mrs. Royal's face clouded over. "Perhaps. You're a better judge of why that is than I, Audrey, because you know all these girls better. But Hope is such a lovely girl, I can't imagine —" She shrugged, then continued, "I suppose it's possible. In New York things like clothes didn't seem to matter, but here I have noticed that it's not always so popular to be different." She smiled at Audrey. "But darling, if that's the reason, it's up to you to help your friends get past those old-fashioned clothes to the real girl underneath."

"What — what do you mean?" Audrey stammered, remembering her secret vow to think of a plan to have Hope join the Secret Six.

Mrs. Royal shrugged. "You know — be a go-between. You can do it, Audrey. And you know what I mean too!"

Audrey did know what her mother meant. And that evening as she lay in bed, she thought of a plan.

She couldn't work out all the details in her mind, but somehow she would arrange it so that the girls from the Secret Six would have to call for her on a day that she went to Hope's house. Once there, they would be forced to see Hope in her own setting, and she was certain they would be as fascinated as she had been on her first visit.

One noontime at school during the following week, Hope asked Audrey if she would like to work on a diorama with her for the school Book Fair.

"What's a diorama?" Audrey asked.

"Well, you take a scene from a book you've read and illustrate it by cutting out figures and scenery and pasting them in a box. It ends up looking like a scene on a stage. Didn't you do them at your school?"

Audrey shook her head. "I never even heard the word before!"

"Oh, they're fun to do, and there are lots of ways of doing them. Some kids use tiny dolls and toy boats and things and glue them in, or you can thumbtack or staple them."

"What kind of box do you use?"

"Usually a shoe box, unless you have a very big, elaborate scene."

"Can you use magazine pictures?"

Hope nodded. "Sure. But I like to draw and color my own, then paste them on cardboard and cut them out."

"It sounds like fun," Audrey said. "Could we draw the clothing on scraps of material and then cut them out and paste them on the figures?"

"That's a wonderful idea!" Hope said. "I never even thought of that."

Audrey couldn't wait to get started, and they decided to go to Hope's house after school that day and start the diorama. In her excitement over the project, Audrey forgot about her Secret Six plans for Hope. But after lunch, she was reminded of them when she ran into Rosie, Lorraine, and Doris.

"Audrey, you're just the one we're looking for!"

"Do you have any magazines at your house?"

"Loads of them — we subscribe to just about everything in print, and —"

"Do you have any old copies we could cut up?"

"About two rooms full!"

"Oh, terrific. Can we come over to your house after school today and start collecting stuff for our hospital scrapbook?" Doris asked.

"Then we can have something to work with at our next meeting. We were just thinking that we ought to get started — you know, get things lined up," Rosie said.

"Wonderful idea," Audrey agreed.

"Is it all right if we all come?" Lorraine asked. "We can bring our own scissors."

Audrey's plans for Hope were whirling around in her head. "Why of course, but — oh!" She slapped her forehead. "I just remembered! I promised Hope I'd go to her house after school today to work on a diorama for the school Book Fair."

The faces fell just as she'd expected, and, according to plan, Rosie said, "What about tomorrow?"

Audrey shook her head. "Sorry, but I have my piano lesson."

"And I have to go to the dentist on Friday," Doris said. They all groaned.

"Gee, couldn't you make it some other time with Hope?" Rosie said.

Audrey shook her head sadly. "Oh, no, I couldn't do that — I already promised." Then she snapped her fingers. "Hey, I have an idea! Suppose you kids come by for me at Hope's house after I've been there a little while? You know, give us a chance just to get *started* on our project. You can say we were all supposed to go to my house to do something special, and I'll pretend I forgot all about it."

71

Lorraine looked at the other two. "It's okay with me. How about you?"

Rosie narrowed her eyes as she told Audrey, "Just be sure you don't say a word to her about our club."

"Oh, of course not! I prom —"

"And you can't bring her along back to your house, either," Doris interrupted, "or we won't be able to do our *club* work."

"I know, I know," Audrey said impatiently, wondering now if her scheme was really going to help — or just make them resent Hope and like her even less.

Audrey and Hope were so absorbed in making the diorama that they didn't hear the doorbell ring, and when Mrs. Miller called to them that some girls had come for Audrey, she jumped up guiltily.

"For me?" She wondered if the note of surprise in her voice sounded as phony to Hope as it did to her, but Hope was so surprised herself that she didn't seem to notice.

The five girls were clustered together in Hope's vestibule, peering about curiously, and Audrey silently prayed that no one would say the wrong thing.

"Audrey, your mother told us you were over

here," Lorraine began. Audrey noticed Mrs. Miller in the background watching, and Mrs. Heinz, Hope's grandmother, in her chair crocheting. "Did you forget about that — project we were supposed to work on at your house?"

Hope turned to Audrey in alarm. "Oh, are you doing a diorama with them too?"

Audrey gasped in fake sudden recollection, as she replied, "No, nothing like that, but — my gosh, I forgot all about it, girls! I'm awfully sorry!" Then, turning to Hope, she explained, "We were supposed to — uh, get some material together for a, uh, special project they have, and I have lots of magazines they want to use, and, uh —"

"It doesn't have anything to do with the Book Fair," Rosie interrupted abruptly, and Joan added, "It's not for anything at school at all."

"What were you two doing?" Doris asked.

"Oh, we're working on this neato diorama of *The Yearling*. Should we show them, Hope?"

Before Hope could reply, they all began begging to see it, and Hope laughed and blushed a little. "It's in my room. Would you like to come up?"

There was a chorus of yesses, and suddenly Mrs. Miller reappeared. "Say, now, aren't you the girls who came on Halloween?" she asked, and as they nodded, Audrey began introducing them to her. Then Hope led them over to her grandmother and repeated the introductions as the old lady peered at them over her glasses, her fingers never stopping their rapid movements as she nodded in acknowledgment.

"Are you crocheting?" Joan asked her politely. When the old woman nodded, she said, "My mother crochets sometimes. Is that a dresser scarf?"

Mrs. Heinz shook her head. "No, now, it's an antimacassar."

There was a strange silence, and the looks that the girls exchanged showed clearly that they were all about to burst out laughing.

"Wh-what's that?" Audrey managed, trying desperately to save the situation.

Hope pointed to the doilies that lay on the tops and arms of all the chairs in the room, replying, "These. They're to keep the furniture from getting dirty."

Suddenly Rosie turned from something she was examining on a table by the far wall to ask, "What is this?" Everyone crowded around a large wooden box with hinges and a long crank handle that hung from its side.

"Why, that's our Victrola," Mrs. Miller said proudly.

"Your *what*?" the girls repeated.

Mrs. Miller opened the lid, and they exclaimed, "A record player!"

It didn't look like any record player Audrey had ever seen, but there was no doubt that it was one.

"But what's this?" Rosie pointed at the handle.

Mrs. Miller chuckled. "This was made before electric phonographs. Look!" She cranked the handle, then swung open the doors of the cabinet that the machine rested on and pulled out a heavy-looking record from the large collection. Carefully, she lifted the machine's large, curving, metal arm, placed the record on the turntable, replaced the arm at the edge of the record, and pushed a lever. The music wasn't like anything Audrey had ever heard before, either — all scratchy and whining, but it had a weird fascination, and the girls were practically hypnotized.

Patsy pointed to a small handle on top of the case. "What's that for?"

"That's a carrying handle. This is one of the first portable phonographs ever made," Mrs. Miller explained. "See?" The record was over, and she removed it, closed the lid, picked up the machine, and handed it to the girls. Rosie accepted it, pretending to collapse from its

75

weight, as she exclaimed, "Wow, it sure is heavy!"

"But — but where do you plug it in?" Doris asked, and the others laughed at her bewildered look.

"Don't you understand, *Dummkopf*? It's not electric," Rosie replied between giggles. "That's why you have to wind it up!"

"Oh," Doris said, still looking confused. "Does it use batteries?"

There was another burst of laughter, and this time even Mrs. Miller and Hope joined in.

They showed the same curiosity about the things in Hope's room, but Audrey noticed them exchanging secret glances that made her feel more and more uneasy. And as she and Hope showed them the work they had done on the diorama, it was obvious that they couldn't have cared less about it and were eager to get back to Audrey's house.

Audrey felt awful for Hope, certain that she was feeling left out. And suddenly, as Audrey gazed at her, she saw how very different Hope looked with her blond hair pulled tight into two long braids, her calico dress with ruffles at the neck and wrists and a hemline that went halfway down her legs, and her brown oxford shoes. It all created a picture of a girl from an old family album — very out of place along-side the other girls with their fluffy shoulder-length hair, bright sweaters, and short skirts. It was funny, she thought now, but lately she'd got used to Hope and hardly noticed how different she looked and dressed. She wondered if she could ever accomplish her club plans for Hope.

The hardest part came at the door. Audrey stood with the other girls saying good-bye to Hope — and not being able to invite her along. She saw the hurt in her friends's serious blue eyes, and she wanted so desperately to say, "Don't worry, I'll make up for it, Hope, you'll see. Before the afternoon is over, they'll be wanting you in our club too." For she *had* accomplished her purpose: they'd met Hope on her own ground, had seen how well she could fit in with them, and what an interesting person she must be. Why, by now, probably, they hardly noticed her strange appearance. And they'd had a wonderful time seeing all the unusual things in her house.

But it didn't work out the way Audrey hoped and planned.

"Isn't that house *something*?" Rosie began as soon as they were clear of it.

Lorraine slapped her hand to her head. "I'd

never have *believed* it if anyone had *told* me!"

"Oh, I would have," Rosie snapped. "After one look at the getups that girl wears!"

Doris shook her head. "I still can't get over that record player."

"I can't get over *everything*!" Patsy said. "That place gave me the *creeps*."

"But it was interesting," Joan said.

"Yeah," Rosie agreed, "like a museum. But who'd want to *live* there?"

Audrey could have cried. But she clenched her fists and made a desperate attempt. "Well, I agree with Joan, it *is* interesting. And maybe none of you would want to live there, but what does that have to do with anything, anyway? I think Hope is a terrific girl, and if you got to know her you'd find out what fun she can be too."

They exchanged one of those looks again, and Audrey gritted her teeth. Instead of helping matters, her plan had really backfired.

"We'll take your word for it," Rosie said. "But just don't get any ideas about her joining our club, or anything, Audrey, because — well, we know you like her a lot, but you have to face the fact that she just doesn't fit in."

Audrey felt awful. She saw now that she had only hurt her cause.

"Hey, here's your house," Rosie was saying. "I haven't been here yet."

Mrs. Royal, Francine, and Sylvia were sitting in the kitchen talking, and Audrey, still in a daze, went through the motions of introducing them.

At the sound of Sylvia's name, another meaningful glance was exchanged among her friends, and Audrey clenched her fists, wanting to scream. It was all getting to be too much — first Hope, now this business with Sylvia. . . .

"Were you girls planning to do something special?" Mrs. Royal asked. Just as Audrey began to shrug, Doris piped up, "We came to look through magazines for stuff for a —" She stopped abruptly, turning red. Rosie had given her a violent nudge which was what had brought the color to her face, but Lorraine finished for her, "A scrapbook or something like that for kids in the hospital." She looked around at the others with one eyebrow raised as if to say, "What else could we do but answer?" Audrey was relieved, because she certainly didn't see any point in lying about it.

"What a really great idea!" Francine cried, turning to Sylvia. "You see, they're not *all* bad."

The girls giggled, but Sylvia said thoughtfully, "I just read an article somewhere about activities like that for kids your age, and it had the most marvelous idea." She turned to

Francine. "It was in one of those magazines we were looking at in the library yesterday. Did you see that one about making activity boxes for sick kids?"

Francine shook her head, "No, I missed that one."

"What is it?" Lorraine asked. All the girls looked interested.

Sylvia frowned. "Let's see — I just glanced through the article, but it explained about making individual activity boxes and putting in them lots of different things for shut-ins to do. You can fill the boxes with all sorts of scraps that you have around the house. Strips of colored papers and beads and pipe cleaners, and things like that, and you take some little plastic containers that pills or toothpicks were in and fill them with paste, and whatever other materials you have around the house that kids can make collages and craft things with."

"Hey, that's a neat idea!" Patsy cried.

"Even better than a scrapbook," Joan declared. "And we can include crossword puzzles —"

"And riddles and cartoons," Rosie said.

"And colored pencils and beads and string," Audrey suggested.

"We can make a whole lot of little boxes so

each kid in the hospital could have one," Patsy said.

"And we could decorate them," Lorraine added.

"What kind of boxes would we use?" Doris asked.

"What about shoe boxes?" Sylvia said. "You must all have some around the house."

"Oh, great!" Joan and Doris said.

"We can put some Christmas decorations in them too," Rosie said. "It's perfect timing."

"And some Chanukah things," Sylvia said, ignoring the sudden silence as she went on, caught up in the girls' enthusiasm. "I've got a whole slew of miniature dreidels that would be *perfect*. My mother had them left over from the bazaar they just had at the temple, and we didn't know what we were going to do with forty-six little dreidels . . ." Her voice dwindled as she looked about at the surprised faces, and when Mrs. Royal cleared her throat, Sylvia burst out laughing and everyone turned red.

"Why, I didn't realize," she said between gulps of laughter, "but you probably don't even know what a dreidel is, do you?"

Francine and Audrey had played the dreidel game with their Jewish friends in New York countless times, but now they exchanged a look, silently agreeing to let Sylvia explain it.

"Well, you see," Sylvia went on, "it's like a little top, and each side has a Hebrew letter that has a certain meaning, and..."

Again, her voice tapered off, but this time Audrey was sure it was because of the closed faces surrounding her, and she burst out, "Oh, I remember, Sylvia! I used to play it with the kids in New York at Chanukah — it's loads of fun! Why don't you show them to the girls?"

Sylvia nodded slowly as Joan said, "Yes, we'd love to see them, wouldn't we?" And all at once, Sylvia's face came to life again, and she said, "Listen, how would you girls like to come to our Chanukah supper? Every year Mother makes a Chanukah supper and we invite all the neighborhood kids to it. Everyone always has a great time." She looked around at them eagerly. "Do you think you'd like to?"

They nodded uncertainly, as Lorraine said, "Well, are you sure it would be okay with your mother?"

"When is it?" Patsy asked.

"Do you mean *all* of us?" Joan said.

Sylvia laughed again now. "Oh, sure, it would be fine with Mother — she loves to have kids in on Chanukah. Anyway, I'll check with her, but it'll be the Sunday before Christmas. You can ask your parents and let me know.

There's plenty of time — it's almost a month away."

"She's sweet," Joan said after Sylvia and Francine left the house to go to the store for Mrs. Royal. "Aren't the activity boxes a great idea?"

"Wasn't it nice of her to invite us to the Chanukah party?" Patsy said. "Do you think her mother really won't mind?"

"I don't think Sylvia would have invited us if she thought her mother wouldn't like it," Audrey answered, and everyone agreed.

"Boy, I didn't even know there was such a thing as a Chanukah party," Doris declared. "As soon as I get home, I'm going to ask my mother if I can go."

Rosie stared at her. "You *are?*"

"Why — why, of course. Aren't you?"

Rosie shrugged, then looked around at the others. "I thought you were all just being polite. You mean you'd actually go to a *Chanukah* party? At *their* house?"

"Why not?" Joan asked. "If we're invited?"

Lorraine glanced at Rosie, then back at Joan. "Well, maybe our folks won't let us."

The others exchanged uncertain glances now too, but Joan said, "Well, anyway, I'm going to ask. It sounds like fun."

"Look, we ought to concentrate on getting

stuff for our activity boxes," Lorraine pointed out, "so we can start working on them at our next meeting."

"Yes," Patsy agreed, "or we'll never have them done in time for Christmas."

"And we have to plan our first fun party too," Doris reminded them.

Now everyone started talking at once, offering suggestions for the party. They decided it would be at Audrey's house on the Friday night after their next meeting. Audrey would provide the records, a dance-instruction book, and the sodas. Rosie offered to bring homemade cupcakes, Joan and Lorraine would bring ice cream, and Patsy and Doris said they'd take care of the potato chips and pretzels.

"Do you think we'll be able to eat all that?" Doris asked, and everyone laughed. By the time they had to leave, the party was all set, but they'd made very little progress on plans for the activity boxes.

"Well, look," Lorraine said, "we're still going to have a meeting before the party, and we can spend all our time on the boxes."

"That's right," Rosie agreed. "Why don't we bring the boxes and all the stuff for them to the next meeting?"

"But that's kind of far away," Doris pointed

out, "and it will be getting pretty close to Christmas."

"Then why can't we just work on them by ourselves *until* the next meeting?" Joan suggested.

"Oh, sure," Patsy agreed. "We can each try to do as many as we can, and get them all together at the meeting."

"And there's no law that says we can't work together between meetings, anyway," Lorraine added, grinning.

"Okay," Rosie agreed. "In secret!"

"I'm going to hunt around for stuff as soon as I get home," said Patsy.

"That's a good idea," Lorraine answered. "And don't forget the little plastic bottles, and paste, and all."

They left in a flurry of plans, excited by the prospect of working on their first project and their first party.

"Say, this was almost like a real meeting," Doris said. "This is *fun*, isn't it?"

"But don't forget," Rosie warned, "we're still the Secret Six. Don't say a word about any of this to anyone."

chapter 6

The remaining leaves floated from the trees in the dismal gray twilight of winter, but December's first snowfall brought days of crisp brightness. The Secret Six were too busy to notice; they were launched and moving full steam ahead on their first projects. Before their next meeting, they had completed many of the activity boxes and were close to their goal of five from each of them.

True to her promise, Sylvia supplied the miniature dreidels, and Audrey was to divide them among the six. They all came over to Audrey's house after school to pick up the dreidels, and were fascinated with spinning them. Audrey asked what they had decided about the

Goldbergs' Chanukah party.

"Oh, I forgot all about it!" Patsy said, but Audrey caught the quick look she exchanged with Rosie. Then she asked Joan, "What about you?"

Joan blushed a little as she replied, "I forgot too. I'll ask my mother today."

Audrey looked directly at Rosie then and said, "Well, I think that if someone is nice enough to invite people to a party, they ought to give that person an answer, even if it's no."

Sylvia had asked Audrey about it earlier that week, and Audrey had been embarrassed to reply that she really didn't know if the other girls were planning to come or not. At that, Sylvia had said, "Oh it's all right. Mother always makes tons of potato *latkes* — pancakes — so five more girls one way or another won't matter. But you and Francine will come, of course?"

"Oh, of course," Audrey had begun, and Sylvia had added quickly, "And Jimmy too?"

Audrey had nodded. "He'd never miss a party — not where there's good food!"

Both girls had laughed; no more was said about the party. Now, having reminded her friends, Audrey decided not to say any more.

Their dance party was such a delightful

secret that the six girls couldn't help whispering about it at school, wanting to discuss every detail together. This soon gave rise to all kinds of rumors. Something special was going on. But as to what, when, or who no one really knew — except that the words "Secret Six" were overheard, and in no time, everyone was asking: "Who are the Secret Six?"

The girls pretended dismay that their club name had leaked out, but they found it awfully exciting to have everyone buzzing about them. By Wednesday, the day of their next meeting, they were so keyed up that they had to caution one another not to make any slips.

And when they met in Patsy's garage that afternoon, and found they'd actually filled thirty activity boxes, they practically flipped out.

"Now we *really* have something to celebrate at our party on Friday!" Joan cried, and everyone agreed.

Hard as it was for the other girls not to make any slips, Audrey was sure it was hardest for her. The others were friendly with just one another. But since she and Hope had become so close, it was a constant effort to keep the promise of secrecy.

Hope couldn't help overhearing the rumors at school, but she never discussed it. That made Audrey quite certain that she knew, but Audrey never dared bring up the subject. Instead, she renewed her secret promise to herself that one of these days she would have Hope in the club.

A driving rain started Thursday night, and continued all day Friday. But the spirits of the Secret Six were not in the least dampened by the weather. If it were still raining that night, the girls decided they would wrap whatever they were bringing in plastic bags.

The rain hadn't shown a sign of letting up by evening. Mr. and Mrs. Royal, about to leave for their bridge game, looked surprised as one dripping girl after another arrived with plastic-wrapped bags.

"What brings you out on a night like this?" Mrs. Royal asked as they hung up their wet coats. Then, eyeing the packages that Audrey quickly snatched away, she added, "What's all that?"

Audrey rolled her eyes in mock pain. "Oh, Mother, don't you remember? I asked you if the girls could come over tonight? You *said* it was all right —"

Mrs. Royal laughed. "Oh, of course, dear. I forgot. I am surprised, though, that they'd bother in all this rain.

Mr. Royal shrugged. "What's a little rain to a bunch of kids? They don't mind it half as much as we do. In fact, Sally, if the Bermans could scare up another couple for their game, I'd gladly stay home by the fire tonight myself."

The girls looked nervously at one another, and Mr. Royal laughed, saying, "Oh, don't worry, we promised we were coming. You'll have the place to yourselves!"

"Oh, *I* know," Mrs. Royal said now. "All that must be those activity boxes you girls have been working on. Gene," she said to her husband, "did I tell you about the marvelous project that Audrey and her friends —"

"Whoa, hold it!" He put a hand on her arm. "You'll tell me on the way to the Bermans. They'll have a fit if we're late."

Audrey waved them off as they ran down to the car, then shut the door with a sigh. "Whew! I thought they'd never leave!"

"Do we have the whole house to ourselves now?" Rosie asked.

"Well, not exactly," Audrey said. "Jimmy and Wimp are in there watching TV — Wimp is sleeping over tonight. Francine and Sylvia are upstairs, but they won't bother us. And I gave Jimmy orders already. We have the basement all to ourselves. Come on, let's go!"

Downstairs, they set about getting the food ready, moving the furniture against the wall, and deciding on which records to play first.

"Look, I found this marvelous dance-instruction book in Francine's room," Audrey said, passing it around to the girls. "She has another one, but that's more complicated. See how it explains all the different steps? And look at these terrific diagrams and pictures, and back here — *hey, who turned off the lights?*" For suddenly, the room was in pitch darkness.

"I'll bet that's my *little brother* Jimmy," Audrey said, gritting her teeth.

"I thought you said they wouldn't bother us!" Patsy exclaimed.

"Wait'll I get hold of him! Now, just stay where you are. I'll have the light on in a minute." Audrey felt her way along the wall. "I know where the light switch is. There's one at the top of the steps that puts the lights on and off down here too, so they must have sneaked — *Hey!*" She kept flicking the switch, but nothing happened. "Something's weird around here."

"I bet it's a fuse," Lorraine said, and now they heard noises from upstairs. The door to the basement opened and a faint beam of light wavered down the steps as Jimmy called, "Hey, you guys, did you blow a fuse or something?"

"Here, give me that," Francine's voice came

to them as the flashlight switched hands. "Are you kids okay down there?"

"Sure," Audrey said. "But we didn't do a thing. All of a sudden the lights just went out!"

"I know," Francine said. "But it couldn't be just a fuse, Jimmy, because there's no electricity *anywhere* in the house. Whenever a fuse blows, it's just the rooms on that fuse that go dark."

"Hey, look!" Wimp called from somewhere upstairs. " It's all dark outside! Even the street lights are out. The houses too — you can't see a thing!"

They heard running footsteps above them and then Francine repeated Wimp's report. "There's not a light anywhere, except when cars go by."

"It's a power failure!" Sylvia exclaimed. "This happened at our house last year during a hurricane. It only hit part of the city, but we didn't have any electricity for a whole day."

"Oh, I remember that," Doris said. "We were lucky. It didn't hit our neighborhood, but it was only a few blocks from us — I guess where Sylvia lives. The whole east end had that power failure."

"Should we phone someone?" Lorraine asked.

92

"Do the phones work?" Audrey called upstairs.

"Let's try," Jimmy said excitedly.

"Wait!" Sylvia called. "Francine, do you have candles in the house?"

"Oh, sure, loads — Mother loves candle-light. There's a pair in the dining room and one in the living room, and, let's see — we've got a box of them, I believe, in the pantry."

As they went to get candles, the Secret Six huddled together in the darkness trying to cheer one another up.

"We can have the party anyway."

"Just think — a party by candlelight!"

"We can eat — we don't need electricity for that."

"And we can still play our records — and dance. It'll be fun!"

"Hey, wait a minute! We can't. It's *electric*!"

"Well, then we can put on the radio. Audrey, do you have a radio?"

"Oh, lunkhead, radios run on electricity too!"

"What about a transistor? Do you have one, Audrey?"

Audrey groaned. "Yes, we have about three of them in the house, but they all need new batteries. We keep forgetting to get them..."

"Besides, suppose we couldn't get the right kind of music? You can't have just any kind of music that comes along when you're learning to dance."

There was silence until Doris piped up. "Well, we can *eat*. That doesn't use up electricity."

Everyone laughed, and suddenly Lorraine snapped her fingers. "Hey, I've got a *super* idea. I think the rain's stopped — why don't we go over and borrow Hope's Victrola? *That* isn't electric."

"Oooh, what a great thought!" everyone cried.

Lorraine laughed. "Really? I was just kidding!"

Audrey could have hugged her. If she herself had been the one to say it, they probably would have brushed it off, but Lorraine had suggested it and they didn't care whether she was joking or not; they loved it. It was the chance she had been waiting for. This would surely open the way to get Hope into the Secret Six.

"Look, kids, I'm all for it." She crossed her fingers. "But — we can't just go over there and ask to borrow that precious Victrola and not invite her back with us."

"Not only that," Patsy pointed out, "but she probably won't lend it to us. After all, maybe the Millers want to use it tonight too, if their power's off."

"Anyhow, what would we tell her?" Rosie asked.

Audrey answered quickly, calculating as she went. "We could just tell her that you kids dropped in tonight and we decided to play some records and then, *wham*, the power failure. We thought of her and her Victrola and figured she might want to come over with it and have some fun with us till the lights go on again."

It didn't take much discussion to convince everyone that this was the perfect solution, and when they got upstairs, after carefully feeling their way in the pitch blackness, there was sudden light. Francine and Sylvia had rounded up six candles and were placing them about when Jimmy burst back in, squealing, "Hey, you guys, guess what! It *is* a power failure! I called the operator, and she told me! And she said not to use the phone unless it was very important. And then you know what? The phone went dead!"

That was a perfect excuse for Audrey and her friends to go over to Hope's house instead of phoning. Francine agreed to their plan, but made them promise to be very careful with the flashlight and come right back.

Jimmy and Wimp pleaded for two candles for Jimmy's room. "We want to play Monopoly. I'll put them on my bedside table, and we'll be so careful, you wouldn't believe it!" Smiling, Francine agreed, and started upstairs with them.

"Isn't this fun?" Rosie said as they hurried toward Hope's house, clinging to one another on the dark sidewalk.

"I've never seen it so dark in my life!" Joan declared.

Audrey was beginning to wonder if they might not have been better off just staying home till the lights came back on, when a man opened the Millers' door and invited them all in. Then he called Hope. In the soft glow of an old-fashioned oil lamp, the living room now looked quaint and charming.

"Daddy, this is my friend Audrey." Hope introduced the other girls to her father, whose warm smile made them feel welcome. Audrey noticed that Hope looked especially nice tonight. She was wearing a sweater, and a skirt that wasn't quite as long as most of her dresses. It was funny, she realized then, that the only time she seemed to notice how Hope looked was when her other friends were around!

Mr. Miller went back to the sofa and his pipe,

and Audrey turned to Hope. "The girls were over at my house when the power went off, so we decided to have a sort of a — little party. You know, with no electricity, we didn't have anything to do. And we thought you might want to come too."

Hope's mouth dropped open slightly as she stared at Audrey. Then she looked slowly around at the other girls, and when she returned her glance to Audrey, she looked as if she'd been given a precious gift.

"And," Rosie put in quickly, "we wondered if you could bring your record player along. You know, the one you don't need electricity for."

"Oh, what a nice idea!" Hope cried, and turned to her father. "May I, Daddy? We'll be very careful with it."

Her father not only let her bring it, but he also insisted on driving them back to Audrey's house. Besides the Victrola, they had to take Hope's records along, because, Mr. Miller pointed out, the machine would play only a certain kind of record that was no longer made.

"My father is going to pick us up at ten o'clock," Lorraine told him as they got out at Audrey's. "He'll be glad to bring Hope home too."

"Ten o'clock?" He frowned. "I don't know about..."

"Oh, please, Daddy, it's Friday, and there's no school tomorrow!"

He grinned at her. "All right. But your mother will probably have my head."

Back down in Audrey's basement, they carefully set the Victrola on the record-strewn table, pushing aside Audrey's useless electric machine and crowding around the curiosity. Each wanted to be the first to wind it up. "Why don't we take turns?" Audrey suggested.

They laughed so much at the winding process and then at the scratchy sound of the music that they almost forgot their plans to learn to dance. But when Lorraine began leafing through the instruction booklet, the others crowded around.

Hope came over and beckoned Audrey back to the Victrola, whispering, "Do you want me to show you how to dance to this?"

Audrey goggled in disbelief. "You mean *you* know how?"

Hope dropped Audrey's hand and started moving gracefully to the music, but as it got faster she began the twisting gyrations that all the teenagers did. The music sounded funny and old-fashioned at first, but it was fast and rhythmic, and Hope was doing the most modern steps to it! And she was *good*. Her pigtails were flying about madly, and her heavy shoes looked almost unreal in the quick steps they were taking.

By now the other girls were standing in a circle around Hope, watching her in awe.

"How did you learn that?"

"Is that really *you*, Hope?"

"Do you take lessons?"

Hope stopped, laughing and shrugging. "I took dancing lessons when I was little — I always loved it. But I learned this from watching TV."

"Really?"

"Will you teach us?"

They all crowded close around her. Hope's cheeks were flushed with excitement, her eyes sparkled. And in that moment, Audrey realized this was *it* — Hope's passport to acceptance by the Secret Six. Surely, now, they would become the Secret Seven!

She closed her eyes, taking a deep breath before suggesting it — and her eyes immediately popped open again in fright, "Hey," she screamed, "I smell *smoke!*"

Everyone began sniffing and looking around with cries of "So do I! But where?" Both candles were still burning steadily and safely. There was no sign of fire.

"Where's the outside door?" Hope asked.

"There isn't one down here. We have to go upstairs, through the house."

They all made a wild dash for the steps, and the smell of smoke became stronger as they did. Audrey, in the lead, flung open the door to the kitchen and was almost overpowered by heavy, stinging smoke. She quickly slammed the door shut as the other girls gasped in terror.

There was a sudden sound of glass breaking down in the basement, and Audrey said, "Shhh!" Then they heard voices calling, "Hurry, girls, come on out through the window!"

They raced back downstairs, as fast as they could in the dim candlelight, and Audrey led them toward a little cellar window in a corner near the ceiling. A large hole had been broken in the glass, and poking through the hole was a frantically waving hand. The hand fumbled around and found the little lever which released the clasp. As the window swung upward toward the girls, they were already climbing up on the couch beneath. Suddenly Sylvia's face appeared at the window.

"Hurry, girls, climb out," she urged them.

As they did, each girl got a helping hand from Sylvia, who was kneeling on the ground outside in a pile of broken glass. Audrey crawled out last, and as she started to rise, she reached to help Sylvia up. It was then she noticed the mass of bleeding cuts on Sylvia's arm.

"Sylvia! Are you all right?"

Sylvia started to rise, then fell over right on top of Audrey. Everyone rushed over, and at that moment, a fire engine careened to a stop before the house, an ambulance right behind it.

The next hours were a nightmare of fear and confusion. Audrey couldn't quite remember when her parents arrived on the scene; she saw them as if in a dream. Everyone who had been in the house was taken to the hospital in the ambulance, with Mr. and Mrs. Royal and their friends and neighbors following along. The firemen went to work to save the house.

It wasn't until much later that the details of what had happened were finally sorted out. By then all those involved in the fire were back safely in their own homes — except for Sylvia. She was suffering from smoke inhalation as well as severe cuts from the broken glass, and had to stay in the hospital.

"Why, I hadn't any idea there was anything

101

wrong with her!" Francine kept saying after the Royals got home. "She ran and got the boys, and when we saw all the smoke in the hallway, I dashed back to the window and started pulling them out onto the grapevine. She scrambled down last. I guess that's how she inhaled all that smoke."

Mr. Royal, an arm around Francine, shook his head. "You two were real heroines. I'm very proud of both of you."

"It was Sylvia's idea to get the girls out through the basement window. As soon as we got down, we went over to it and she just smashed it in to get at the lock."

"How did you get yourselves and the boys down the grapevine?" Mrs. Royal asked. "That was brilliant!"

"It was really neat!" Jimmy exclaimed. "We felt just like Tarzan, climbing down those crazy vines."

Francine smiled for the first time. "Some Tarzans! Their eyes were absolutely running from the smoke. So were ours. I climbed out first, and Sylvia just grabbed Jimmy and handed him down to me. I got down with him and then went back and she gave me Wimp. After we were on the ground, she came scrambling out herself and crawled down. It was only the second floor, but for a while there, it seemed like the top of the Empire State Building!"

Mrs. Royal hugged Jimmy and Audrey to her. She looked down at them, blinking very hard. "I don't know if you realize how lucky we all are."

Audrey shook her head. "Lucky! I'll never forget that smoke!"

"What's so lucky?" Jimmy said mournfully. "I don't have a bed — or a room to sleep in anymore."

"It's just a miracle that the house didn't burn down," Mr. Royal told him. "Don't worry, son, your room will be back in shape by the weekend, and you'll have a brand-new mattress too."

That had been the source of the fire. They figured out that while Jimmy and Wimp were absorbed in their game, one of them must have knocked over one of the candles without realizing it, and the candle had continued to burn lying on its side — they hadn't even noticed it. But it must have ignited the mattress, because as soon as the boys smelled smoke they saw it was coming from the mattress. That was when they discovered the candle lying on its side, still burning away. But the bed had caught fire so quickly that by the time the boys discovered the candle, a heavy stream of smoke was pouring out of the mattress. Sylvia and Francine, in the bedroom next door, smelled the smoke and rushed in to rescue them.

During the hours they waited at the hospital, Mr. Royal came back briefly to the house to check on things. By then, the fire had been put out; in fact, the mattress itself was outside, a charred and water-soaked wreck. By that time, power had been restored. Mr. Royal had opened all the windows in the house, so when they finally got back from the hospital, the smoke was gone — except for the smoky odor, especially in Jimmy's room.

"You'll sleep in the other bed in Audrey's room until your room is fixed up," Mrs. Royal told Jimmy. Before he could burst out in the fury that showed on his face, his mother added sternly, "Let's not hear a word of complaint about it. Just be thankful that you're alive and unhurt."

Jimmy's mouth hung open for a moment, then he slumped suddenly and said, "All right. And I'm sorry about everything. We tried to be careful — honest! Gosh, I feel terrible about Sylvia. I deserve to be in the hospital instead of her!"

Mr. Royal patted his arm. "Don't be foolish, Jimmy. Nobody wants to see *anyone* in the hospital. It *was* an accident."

"Do you think Sylvia will be all right in time for the Chanukah party? Will she be home by then?" Audrey asked.

"The doctor said that if everything goes well, she should be home in a few days."

"Oh," Francine said, "I feel so *relieved!* She really was fantastic. When I saw that the window was locked, I didn't know *what* to do. But she just smashed it — with her bare fist!" Francine made a fist and stared at it.

"She's a brave girl," her father said. "And now, folks, let's all go to bed. And say a prayer of thanks that no one was seriously hurt."

As they went upstairs, Audrey assured Francine, "Sylvia's going to be all right, I know she is. And she's going to have the biggest and best party ever!"

chapter 7

By Monday morning, the whole school was buzzing with stories of the fire. Some claimed that the girls who met at Audrey's must be the Secret Six and that they had started it. Others said it was because of the power failure. Some even said that Jimmy and Wimp were playing with matches. Word went around that Sylvia had everything from third-degree burns to pneumonia. Other tales about the Secret Six were so wild that the club, and the girls, again took on the character of troublemakers.

Before noon dismissal, each of the Secret Six was summoned to Mr. Marshall's office. Hope was called down also.

"I know it was an accident," the principal began, "because I heard the whole story on Saturday. And by this evening, everyone in town will know the truth because the *Jupiter Gazette* will have the facts in the afternoon paper. But I just wanted to — er, check with you girls and find out if there is anything else I ought to know." He looked at them with a smile so friendly that they relaxed for the first time since they had entered his office, but each looked to the other to reply.

Finally, Audrey said, "Well, what would you like to know?"

Mr. Marshall shrugged. "Since I spoke to Mr. Royal and Mrs. Goldberg and found out how the whole thing *really* happened, I suppose the only thing I don't know is about this — this talked-of club of yours. I don't like to probe, but in the light of what has happened — this, following that little incident at Halloween — I'm afraid you'll have to let me in on your secrets."

Rosie screwed up her face, looking as if she were going to cry, and blurted out, "See, I *told* you they would think the worst of us just because of that trouble at Halloween! Why — why, that's the reason we *started* our secret club in the first place." And she went on to explain their purpose and their plans, trembling as she finished. "It's not true — all the awful things everyone is saying about us!"

"We just wanted to — to do some good, and have some fun together," Patsy added, and all the other girls nodded.

Mr. Marshall smiled and then nodded too. "It looks as if you had been misjudged, girls. I'm sorry. That should teach us adults a good lesson about jumping to conclusions."

"Oh, *we've* learned a *lot* from this experience!" Lorraine exclaimed, glancing at Hope.

"We sure have," Doris agreed.

"And you've come a long way in a short time," Mr. Marshall said. "I'm interested in those activity boxes. Suppose you bring one to school after lunch and show it to me."

"Oh, we can bring them all," Joan offered. "We planned to deliver them to the hospital today, anyway."

"Fine! Then bring them to the office after lunch and I'll keep them safe here for you until after school. In fact" — and he snapped his fingers — "I'll drive you over to the hospital myself! I wanted to visit Sylvia, anyway. A lovely girl."

"And a real hero!" Rosie declared.

"Heroine," Joan whispered, and everyone laughed.

"You know," Lorraine added, "it was Sylvia

who told us about the activity boxes. She explained how to make them too."

Mr. Marshall nodded. "That sounds like Sylvia. Now, just one more thing. If you *are* the Secret Six — well, maybe I can't count correctly anymore, what with the new math, but there are seven of you here . . ."

"You see . . ." Doris began breathlessly, and then she launched into the story of Hope and her Victrolia.

When she finished, Rosie said, "But we're not the Secret *Six* anymore. Some of us talked about it over the weekend, and we didn't vote on it or anything yet, but we wanted to change it to the Secret Seven and ask Hope to join. That is" — and she looked around at the other girls, finally settling her gaze on Audrey — "if everyone agrees." Then she smiled at Hope. "And if you want to. But we hope you do, don't we, girls?"

At that, they all shouted "Yes!" Audrey, sitting beside Hope, squeezed her hand. Hope had turned beet-red, but before she could reply, Mr. Marshall said, "All right girls, you can conduct your personal business afterward. And" — the note of sternness dissolved in his warm smile — "if this is the kind of business your club is conducting, you have my blessing. Even though" — and he cleared his throat as he examined his folded hands — "we don't generally approve of secret clubs."

"It sure isn't secret anymore," Patsy said, as the others laughingly agreed.

"Case dismissed," Mr. Marshall said jokingly. "It's time for lunch, so you may all go home now. And bring those boxes back with you."

Hope stopped by for Audrey and helped her carry hers back. Hope's eyes sparkled as she told Audrey, "I told my mother and grandmother about the club, and they said all right, since you're all such nice girls. I just have to get final permission from Daddy, but I know he'll say yes. Isn't that wonderful?"

"Oh, yes, Hope!"

As they grabbed each other and whirled around on the sidewalk, Audrey was silently congratulating herself that the promise she'd secretly made to get Hope into the club had come true. And then, she realized, she really hadn't been the one to accomplish it. It had just happened. . . .

Mr. Marshall had another surprise for the club members. That afternoon, he called a special all-school assembly. Then he proceeded to explain that he wanted to put a stop to all the wild stories circulating around school about the Secret Six. He wanted everyone to know what actually happened at the Royals' house on Friday and what the girls involved were really doing. He displayed some of the activity boxes they had made, explained what they were for, and then asked the girls responsible for them to stand up.

Audrey gripped the edge of her chair, unable to move. But when she saw Rosie pop up, then Lorraine, then Patsy and Doris together, she nudged Joan, seated beside her. They both rose slowly to a swell of enthusiastic applause. Audrey's cheeks were burning, and she saw that Joan was blushing too. As they turned to smile at each other, Audrey had a wonderful feeling of warmth for her fellow club members and for all the boys and girls in school who were clapping for them.

Later, they delivered their boxes to the hospital, with Mr. Marshall as their special escort, and received warm thanks and compliments for their work.

"I guess our idea worked pretty well after all!" Rosie exclaimed on the way back home. "Gee, I wish they had let us see Sylvia."

"Me too," Patsy said. "But Mr. Marshall promised to tell her all about what happened today, and how everyone knows the activity boxes were her idea."

When do you think they'll let her come home?" Joan asked.

"Last night Francine spoke to Sylvia's mother, and she thinks by Wednesday," Audrey replied. "She's much better. Francine visited her twice already, and she'll probably go again this evening."

"I hope she got our cards," Rosie said.

"She should have received them today," Audrey said. "By the way, Mrs. Goldberg is still planning to have that Chanukah party. Remember — the one Sylvia invited us to?"

They nodded, looking at one another and trying to avoid Audrey's eyes. Finally Lorraine said, "We — we'd love to go, if she still wants us."

"Oh, of course she does!" Audrey cried.

"In fact," Lorraine said then, "I was thinking it would be nice if, instead of sending her a present in the hospital the way our mothers suggested, we could each bring something for her to the party."

"Why don't we make something for her?" Joan suggested. "That would show her — well, you know . . ."

Audrey smiled. "That we cared enough about her to make something special instead of just going out and buying something?"

Joan nodded eagerly, and Patsy said, "Oh, yes, let's!"

"But what shall we make?"

"Activity boxes!" Rosie said, and everyone laughed.

"No, honest, what could we make for her?" Lorraine said.

"Do you mean like a cake or something?" Doris asked.

Lorraine giggled. "Why do you always think about food? No, silly — though I guess you could do that too. But Joan meant something like a bookmark, or an apron — you know, something she can keep."

"Oh, that's a wonderful idea," Doris said, "but I can't make any of those things!"

Patsy explained, "Well, then, choose something you can make. Hair bows, or a string of beads..." Her voice trailed off, and she frowned in thought. "You know, come to think of it, I don't know what to do, either."

"Look, let's have a club rule right now," Lorraine said. "We each have to make a Chanukah present for Sylvia. But if we absolutely can't think of something to make, or just can't do it, it's okay to buy something. How does that sound?"

"Suppose we say," Audrey amended, "if we buy something, we have to make the card to go with it?"

"Can we make something and make the card?" Patsy asked.

"Oh, sure," Joan said. They all agreed on the rules, and Audrey promised to tell Hope about it too, for Francine had reported that Sylvia wanted Hope to come to the party.

At dinner, Francine announced that Sylvia was doing so well she would be able to come home on Wednesday. "And by the way, Audrey," she added, "Mrs. Goldberg still doesn't know if you and your friends are coming to the Chanukah party."

"We're all coming," Audrey said. "The girls just told me today. I'll call Mrs. Goldberg after dinner and tell her."

It was the first time Audrey had talked to Mrs. Goldberg and she felt immediately at ease with her. "I'm delighted you girls can come," she told Audrey. "And tell your friends we've decided to keep the party a surprise for Sylvia this year. We're going to tell her we're skipping the party for the neighborhood because we think it would be too much excitement for her. That we'll have just the family." She giggled. "I know she'll put up a big fuss, because she aways loves it so, but that should make it even more fun — I hope!"

"Is there anything we can do to help?" Audrey asked.

"I'm going to ask Francine to keep Sylvia

occupied while we make the preparations. If she can spend the whole afternoon at your house, we can all grate our knuckles off."

"Huh?"

Mrs. Goldberg laughed. "Well, after all, it *is* Chanukah, and for that we always have tons of potato *latkes* — that's Yiddish for pancakes. And so you have to grate tons of potatoes for them."

"Oh, we could certainly help you with that," Audrey assured her.

"It's not easy," Mrs. Goldberg said.

"But we'd love to! I know the girls would. Suppose we all bring potato graters and help? You'll need lots of help with a gang like that."

"That's really sweet of you, Audrey. If you're sure..."

Audrey was never so busy, nor had she ever had so much fun in her life. Christmas Eve was only a week after the party, and between preparations for that and for Sylvia's Chanukah presents, everyone was frantically busy. Audrey planned to make a handkerchief with the crocheted edging that Hope had taught her, but the girls had decided not to tell one another what their gifts would be. And they were all eager to help Mrs. Goldberg grate the "tons of potatoes."

chapter 8

By the Sunday of the Goldbergs' party, Christmas was definitely in the air. This was especially true of the Royals, for they had decided to go out in the country and get their tree that morning so they could have Sylvia come over in the afternoon to help decorate it and stay until early evening.

"It seems funny having a tree so long before Christmas," Jimmy remarked as they carried it into the house.

"It should seem funny to you to be helping to get the tree," Mr. Royal remarked. "After all, up until last year you thought Santa Claus brought it, all decorated."

"Aw, that's baby stuff!" Jimmy cried indignantly. "It's much more fun getting it and decorating it yourself."

"Now do you see what you missed out on all these years?" Audrey teased. "I used to be downstairs helping with the lights while you were up in your bed dreaming about Santa Claus. Boy, you sure missed the fun!"

"So did you," Francine said, grinning. "All the years I helped Mother and Dad alone. Those were the days!"

Everyone laughed, buoyed up by the festive spirit that had swept over them when they arrived at the field of Christmas trees. Each looked for the tallest and fullest tree, then argued the good points of their choice. Finally, they narrowed it down to two, and made the final decision. Then it became a treasure hunt as they went up to the attic to find the boxes of lights and decorations, and bring them down to the living room. Each time someone unwrapped a favorite ornament from its tissue, there was a shout of joy.

"No decorating till Sylvia gets here!" Francine warned them as Jimmy examined strings of lights longingly.

Mr. Goldberg drove Sylvia over at about two o'clock, and everyone swarmed around to embrace her — even Jimmy! She looked a little thinner, but her cheeks were aglow with excitement, and Mrs. Royal brought out apples and nuts as they all set about decorating the tree.

"This is super!" Sylvia cried. "I've never done this in my life. Oh, look at these lovely things!" She carefully picked up a tiny carved angel, painted the color of ivory and trimmed with gold paint and red velvet.

"A Danish friend in New York gave us that one year," Francine explained. She turned to Audrey. "Do you remember? That was when you had that terrible case of chicken pox."

"Oh, yes!" Audrey exclaimed, remembering. And as Sylvia unwrapped a tiny Limoges china madonna, she said, "Antoinette — Francine's French friend — brought that to us from France."

Both girls continued to explain the history of each ornament as they unwrapped them one by one from their protective tissue. Jimmy busied himself helping his father string up the lights. Many of the decorations were simple and crude, made by the Royal children over the years and packed away carefully each year, remembered and cherished again the next Christmas.

Sylvia constantly exclaimed and marveled over the ornaments. Just as they started putting the colored balls on the tree, the doorbell rang. Audrey jumped up and hurried to answer it, knowing it would be her friends and wanting to remind them not to give away the secret of the party to Sylvia.

They were all there, including Hope, each with a potato grater and a brightly-wrapped gift. These Audrey quickly put on the closet shelf as the girls went in to see the tree.

"Oh, it's *gorgeous!*" they exclaimed. Then, catching sight of Sylvia on her knees on the other side of the tree, they ran over and swooped down on her, almost knocking her over.

"Sylvia! How are you?"

"When did you get home?"

"How do you feel?"

They sat around her, cross-legged, all talking at once. Soon they were examining the decorations too, and when Francine broke open the packages of tinsel they cried, "Oooh, can we help?" Francine smiled at them as she handed each girl some tinsel, saying, "Okay, you can each toss on a handful."

"That's all we really have time for," Doris said, consulting her watch. As the others shot her a warning look, she added quickly, "We have somewhere to go."

Sylvia shook her head in wonderment as they threw the tinsel on the tree. "This certainly is a colorful holiday, isn't it?" Her smile faded as she added, "It must be fabulous, coming down on Christmas morning and seeing lots of beautiful packages around the tree."

"We try not to lose sight of the serious part of Christmas," Mr. Royal put in now. "After all, it *is* a religious holiday."

Mrs. Royal added smoothly, "But you're right, Sylvia, it is a beautiful time of year."

"I know some people who don't even get a tree at Christmas," Hope said. "They spend most of their time at church and everyone gets just one gift."

"The kids too?" Jimmy asked, and Hope nodded. "Oh, boy, they must be awful poor — or crazy," he said.

Mrs. Royal shook her head at him sadly. "That must be just what they think of us, Jimmy — poor in spirit, and foolish and child-like. We have come a long way from the meaning of Christmas, haven't we?"

"I don't see anything wrong with all of this," Sylvia said, indicating the tree, "if you keep what's important about the holiday in your heart. I think it's very touching the way you keep all these little ornaments that have their own special meanings and memories for you. Those things are part of the spirit of Christmas too, aren't they?"

The seven girls discussed this on the way to the Goldberg house.

"I felt sorry for Sylvia," Patsy said. "There she was with all that Christmas stuff, and all they do on their holiday is light candles and get presents."

"Yes," Doris said, "and by the time Christmas day comes, Chanukah is usually over, and all their fun is over too, just when most everyone else is starting theirs."

"I know some Jewish people who get a gift on each night of Chanukah," Lorraine said. "Boy, I wouldn't say that's so bad! I think there are eight nights."

"Really?"

"Do all Jews do that?"

"No," Audrey replied, "my friends in New York didn't. They just got them on the first night."

"Well," Rosie said, changing the subject and looking around at everyone with a twinkle in her eyes, "since Hope told us she was joining, we've never had a chance to talk about it together. So how about a cheer now for the Secret *Seven?*"

There was a burst of laughter as Doris said, "Some secret!"

"Never mind!" Lorraine snapped. "We still can *have* secrets, even if everyone does know *who* we are!"

"Right," Rosie agreed. "Like what we *do*."

"And when we meet," Patsy interrupted.

"And where," Joan added.

"And it's going to be just as much fun." Patsy smiled and nodded.

"More," Lorraine corrected her, glancing over at Hope as she explained. "Now that Hope is a member, she can teach us lots of things —"

"Like how to dance!" Doris cried.

"And we can use her Victrola whenever there's a power failure," Rosie said, to everyone's laughter.

By now they had reached Sylvia's house; Mrs. Goldberg answered the door.

"Well," she exclaimed at seeing the girls with their graters, "you really are prepared to work! It's so nice of all of you. Sylvia will be thrilled."

"Do you have a special place where you keep gifts?" Lorraine asked. "We all brought something for Sylvia —" They held out their packages, and Mrs. Goldberg gasped in surprise. "Oh, my, how lovely! Here, give them to me. I'll put them away."

122

The house was rich with the aroma of cooking, and as Steven and Bobby scurried past with armloads of dishes, Mrs. Goldberg explained, "They're setting up the buffet."

In the kitchen, she introduced them to her mother, who was seated at the counter peeling potatoes.

"Oh, we can do that," Audrey said, as she eyed the mound of potatoes. "Why don't half of us peel and the other half grate?"

"Fine," Mrs. Goldberg said. "Mother and I can get started mixing the pancake batter right now, and then begin the frying. By that time, you should have another batch ready for us to mix up."

They chattered happily as they worked, and when Steven and Bobby finished their jobs of setting up, they wanted to join the cooking party too. But Mrs. Goldberg laughingly turned them away, saying, "You go keep Grandpa company. Ask him if the wax is cleaned out of the menorah from last night, and if not, there's a job for you." She turned to the girls, explaining, "This is the fourth night of Chanukah, so that means we light five candles altogether. Have you girls ever been to a Chanukah celebration before?"

Except for Audrey, they all shook their heads, and Mrs. Goldberg exclaimed, "Oh, how

123

wonderful! We love being able to explain everything for the first time."

Mrs. Goldberg and her mother chatted with the girls as they all worked together. As Mrs. Goldberg put the last batch in the oven to keep warm for the supper, she gave each girl a pancake and took one for herself. "Your reward for all your hard work!"

They exclaimed in delight, after tasting, and were full of compliments for the cooks. "Why are these especially for Chanukah?" Joan asked, licking her fingers.

"Probably because they're so scrumptious!" Doris said.

"That's always a good reason," Mrs. Goldberg laughed. "Mother, I've forgotten — what is the reason for *latkes* on Chanukah?"

"Well, the story goes that when the Maccabees — those were the Jewish soldiers fighting the Syrians' oppression — were in pursuit of the enemy, they asked the women in one of the villages they were passing through to feed them, for they were very hungry. But they told the women they must be very quick, there was no time to lose, so the women made them pancakes. It was the quickest food they knew how to make."

"No wonder the Maccabees won!" Audrey

said. "An army fed on food like this could be inspired to win any battle."

The girls were tired after their bout with the potatoes — each had had a turn at the grating, learning quickly that it was no easy job and one that left its mark — scraped kunckles — on the inexperienced. Now they jumped at Mrs. Goldberg's suggestion of relaxing in the living room for the half hour that was left before the party.

Bobby was playing checkers with his grandfather, while Steven and his father lounged on the sofa watching an undersea adventure on TV. The girls looked about curiously. At one end the entire wall was covered with bookshelves. A baby grand piano filled one corner. Patsy whispered, "Where are the Chanukah things?"

Everyone shrugged, and Audrey replied, "I guess everything is in the dining room, because that's where the party is going to be."

Doris shook her head, murmuring, "I sure don't see how it can be any fun without a tree or window decorations or wreaths or anything."

The doorbell rang and Mrs. Goldberg asked one of the boys to answer it. When Bobby opened the door, Audrey could see Wimp and Clifford standing on the porch. Wimp was handing a big box to Bobby, who turned around and called, "Mom, some kids came with something for you."

Mrs. Goldberg hurried to the door and invited them in. Then she took the box Wimp was still holding out.

"My mother wanted you to have it for your holiday," he told her, twisting his fingers. "She said to tell you — to tell you she wishes all of you a — happy holiday, and she'll — we'll — never forget how brave Sylvia was, and all." The red in his face crept to his ears as he added, "Can I see her?"

"She isn't home yet, but she'll be back soon. We're having a Chanukah supper and we were hoping you'd come. Why don't you both take off your coats and stay for the party? We'd love to have you!"

Suddenly, Steven and Bobby came over and stood very close to their mother, casting sour looks at the boys.

Wimp looked directly at each of them, smiling uncertainly as he gave a funny half-wave. "Hiya. Remember us? We met you over at Jimmy's."

Steven stuck out his chin. "My sister saved your *life*."

Wimp's smile quavered. "Yeah. She did."

"What's in that box?" Bobby asked.

"A fruit cake. It's my mother's specialty. She only makes them at Christmas." He blushed again. "But it's for any time. . . ."

Mrs. Goldberg bent down a little toward the boys. "Come on, boys, take off your coats and join us. You'll have a good time." They exchanged a questioning look, then glanced into the living room and caught sight of the girls. Soon they were taking off their wraps, and Audrey smiled at the suits, white shirts, and ties they wore, wondering if they just *happened* to be dressed up that way on the day of the Chanukah party . . .

The doorbell rang again, and this time it was Jimmy, carrying a gaily wrapped package almost as big as himself.

"It's for Sylvia," he replied to everyone's questions about it, "and I'm not telling what it is." He walked straight over to Steven and Bobby, and Audrey caught her breath as she heard him say, "Hi, Steven. Hi, Bob. Hey, how about coming over to my house after Christmas? I think I'm getting trains, and we can play with them together."

"We got a racing-car set for Chanukah!" Bobby said proudly. "Want to see it?" He included Wimp and Clifford in the offer, but Mrs. Goldberg stopped all of them. "No, don't go downstairs now, boys — you'lll play with it later. Sylvia's going to be here any minute. Let's turn out all the lamps but one, so she won't see you before she gets into the room."

"Why don't we all go in the dining room and you bring her in there," someone said.

"Oh, yes, and we'll keep it dark and yell surprise when she comes in!"

"And turn on the lights, and she'll see all the kids and the party set-up!"

They hurried into the dining room and grouped themselves in the corner behind the door as Mr. Goldberg turned out all the lights but one lamp in the living room.

chapter 9

"Shhh, I think they're coming!"

There was some noisy wriggling around, followed by bursts of laughter and streams of shushing. Then, a sudden silence, breathless waiting — and nothing happened! Another burst of nervous laughter, another hiss of shushing, a quavering silence, and then — footsteps on the porch! The door opened, and Sylvia and Francine entered, talking together. Mrs. Goldberg greeted them, and then said, "Sylvia, would you go and see if I left my glasses in the dining room? There's a program I wanted to watch..."

"A program?" Sylvia repeated indignantly.

"I'm *hungry*! Aren't we going to eat soon? Didn't Grandma and Grandpa get here yet? M'mm, what do I smell?" She started for the dining room, feeling for the light switch as she added, "It smells deli —"

"SURPRISE!"

The shriek went up the moment the lights blazed on, and Sylvia looked a bit dazed, to everyone's delight. She really was surprised! "I never guessed," she said to Francine. "And doesn't it look festive!"

The dining-room table, heaped with platters of food, napkins, dishes, and silver, had been pushed against the wall. In the center stood a large brass candelabra, its intricate carvings glistening against the gleaming metal that had been carefully polished.

Sylvia shook her finger playfully at her mother and father. "And you said no Chanukah party this year — it would be too much for me!" She ran over and hugged them, her face aglow. Then, catching sight of the bright mound of packages heaped on the sideboard, she asked, "What in the world is *that?*"

"Chaunkah presents to you from the Secret Seven!" the girls chorused.

"And *me!*" Jimmy squealed, patting the enormous package that stuck way out over the edge.

Wimp looked around on the table and, finding the fruit cake set out on a gold-bordered plate, he brought it over to Sylvia. "My mother made this for your holiday."

Sylvia's mouth had dropped open, and now, looking around at all of them, she shook her head. "Why, I can't believe it! How absolutely fabulous!"

"Boys and girls," Mr. Goldberg said, "we'll begin now. We will have the lighting of the candles, with perhaps a little explanation and history — and then the party."

Steven and Bobby passed skullcaps to their father and grandfather, and as they put on their own, Mr. Goldberg explained that these yarmulkes were worn by men and boys during all religious ceremonies. Then, pointing to the candelabra on the table, he said, "And this is the menorah, which has nine candle holders."

"But I thought Chanukah lasted only eight days," Jimmy said.

Mr. Goldberg smiled. "That's right. The ninth one — this one," and he pointed to the holder which stood above the other eight, right in the center, "is for the special lighter candle, called the *shamos*."

"Oh," Lorraine said, "I see — you light one candle for each night."

"Right," said Mr. Goldberg. "You start with

one and each night light one more. And always with the lighter shamos."

"Which night is this?" Wimp asked.

"The fourth," replied Bobby.

"Oh — then you light five tonight," said Clifford.

"It must be pretty on the last night," Lorraine said.

"It is," Sylvia replied. "You can come over and see if you like."

"Let's see," Rosie mumbled, "in four more days — say, now, that'll be nearly Christmas!"

"Right again," said Mr. Goldberg. "And though each holiday is a joyous celebration, the reasons are quite different. Did you know that on Chanukah Jews celebrate their victory in the first religious war in history?"

His audience was intrigued and he went on to tell about the war between the Jews and Syrians, explaining how the Syrians wanted the Jews to worship their idols, and when they refused, took over their Temple and desecrated it; how the great patriot leader, Judas Maccabeus, led a small but courageous army of the Maccabees against the mighty Syrian forces, won the battle, and retook their temple.

"And the reason we light this menorah as we do," he concluded, "is that when the Jews returned to the temple to restore it, they discovered there were only a few drops of oil left to keep the lights burning. But, miraculously, the lights burned on for eight days, just time enough for more oil to be prepared. And so, Chanukah is celebrated for eight days."

The group listened, fascinated at Mr. Goldberg's explanation, and now they watched wide-eyed as Mrs. Goldberg handed Sylvia a small box of candles. Sylvia chose five, all different colors, and placed them in the menorah, four in the regular holders and the fifth one in the special high place. Then someone turned off the lights, and her grandfather handed her a lighted match with which she lit the shamos candle. Mr. Goldberg tapped Bobby's shoulder, indicating that he should light the next one, and carefully Bobby lifted the lighted candle, touched it to the wick of the first one in line, and when its light flared, handed the lighter candle to his brother, who lit the second candle. Mr. Goldberg took it from him and handed it to Wimp, saying, "Would you like to light the next one?"

Wimp's face lit up with pleasure as he touched the flame to the third candle. Jimmy was given the fourth to light, and as he did so, the girls exclaimed at the loveliness of the lighted menorah in the darkened room. The two men began chanting the Hebrew blessing, joined by the rest of the Goldberg family. Then the lights were turned back on, Mr. Goldberg placed the menorah high on the china cabinet for safety's sake, and everyone began talking. The two women now went into the kitchen, and returned moments later with huge platters of potato pancakes.

It was a wonderful party. The pancakes disappeared almost as fast as they were brought in, and there was turkey and roast beef and salad, punch and nuts, and Wimp's fruit cake. By the time everyone finished eating, the table looked almost as full of food as it had at the beginning, and Mrs. Goldberg warned them, laughing, "If you don't eat more, you'll have to come back tomorrow to help us finish it."

But they were no longer interested in food. The girls helped clean up, as Steven and Bobby took out their dreidels and began spinning them, showing the boys how to play. Their grandfather put down shiny pennies as prizes to be won. The girls soon joined them and as they all sprawled on the living-room floor, Sylvia went over to the piano and began a tune, soon sung by the Goldberg family and quickly joined by the rest:

Dreidel, dreidel, dreidel,
I made it out of clay.
When it's dry and ready,
Dreidel I shall play — oh!

They swung into the next chorus with more verve, and sang it over and over again until voices began dropping off. Then Sylvia stopped and announced, "I'm going to open my presents now."

Wimp turned to Steven and Bobby. "What about you? Are you going to open yours?"

"Oh," Bobby answered, "we all got our presents on the first night of Chanukah. Hey, we were going to go down and play with my new racing set — remember?"

"Why don't you wait till Sylvia opens the things?" Mrs. Goldberg said.

"We got baskets for our bikes too," Steven said.

"And cowboy shirts with real fringes..."

"And checkers, and Parcheesi..."

"Wow!"

"That's neat!" commented the other boys.

"And," added their grandfather, handing the brothers an enormous box wrapped in blue paper covered with little silver menorahs, "this, from Grandma and me." At the same time, his wife brought in a small, narrow package and handed it to Sylvia. She carefully undid the wrappings and revealed a white satin box. Inside, on a green velvet cushion, lay a gleaming, delicate gold chain. She held it up for everyone to admire. Francine fastened it around Sylvia's neck, and Sylvia exclaimed, "Oh, Grandma, Grandpa, it's so beautiful! Thank you so much!" And she kissed them both.

Now a yell went up from her brothers, who had just unwrapped their package to find a huge, electrified world globe. They ran to plug it into the nearest outlet, and everyone crowded around to study the lighted globe.

"Boy, I hope I get one of those for Christmas!" Wimp cried.

"Me too," Clifford said. Then, turning to the Goldberg boys, he added, "But what do you do on Christmas?"

They looked at him in bewilderment. "What do you mean?" Bobby asked.

"I mean, by the time Christmas comes, you've had all your presents already and your fun is all over — and that's when ours is just starting."

Steven looked puzzled, and said, "But Christmas isn't *our* holiday. *Chanukah* is."

"Don't you," his brother retorted, "feel left

out on Chanukah when all the Jewish kids get their presents and you don't get anything?"

Wimp and Clifford looked at each other, then answered together with a grin, "No, because it's not *our* holiday," and chortled.

Now the girls clustered around Sylvia as she began opening her packages from them. She admired each handmade card, and read off the rhymed good wishes.

Some of the girls had been able to draw illustrations; others had made simple designs or used star stamps in different colors. Sylvia showed each card, then opened the gift it had come with. And each girl had managed to make a gift, after all.

Rosie's was a pencil holder, made from an ordinary can that she had painted, lacquered, and decorated with tiny seashells, buttons, and sequins. Lorraine had made an "Everything Holder" — a string of many-colored felt pockets to hold things like hankies and scarves, that Sylvia could hang from a hook. Joan had made a letter caddy in the form of a girl with outstretched hands, fashioned from a wire hanger bent to shape, covered with fabric, and enhanced with a paper face. Doris gave her a little oval dish made of mosaic tiles. Patsy's gift was a small wood picture frame decorated with tiny artificial flowers, pearls, and colored beads. Hope's was a yellow organdy kerchief appliquéd all over with yellow-centered white daisies. And Audrey gave her a handkerchief of white linen crocheted with a green edging.

Finally, Sylvia opened Jimmy's package. He stood close by, nearly bursting with excitement. As Sylvia tore off the large sheets of colored tissue, a shout of surprise went up. It was an easel.

She stared at it is amazement. "*You* didn't make this?"

"Well, not exactly," Jimmy confessed. "When we moved in, I found this broken-down old easel in the attic —"

Audrey and Francine exchanged a smile of sudden recollection. "You don't mean that this is —" Francine began, and Jimmy nodded vigorously.

"Yup. I repaired the whole thing — it was all coming apart. Half the nails were rusty or missing, and I put it together again with all new nails and a new chain, and I sanded it down and then I stained it."

Sylvia gave him a big hug. Then she looked around at everyone, laughing as she said, "I — I just don't know how to thank you. You're all absolute angels, and I don't think I'll ever forget this as long as I live!"

"And to think," her grandmother exclaimed, "that you all made these things by yourselves! Why, it's just splendid."

"Well," Rosie said, "we wanted Sylvia to have something special from each of us..." She faltered, and Lorraine went on, "To show her how much we appreciate what she did for all of us."

"And, Sylvia, because you're so nice!" Doris added.

"Yeah," Wimp said, and everyone smiled.

"Oh my!" said Sylvia, blushing. "I don't know what to say — except, Wimp, please tell your mother thank you for the fruit cake. It's absolutely delicious."

"She's going to make you one every year," he replied solemnly. "And she said to say thank *you* from our whole family." Turning quickly to Bobby and Steven, he muttered, "Could we play with that racing set now?"

But Sylvia put a hand on his shoulder and added, "You know, I didn't do any more than Francine, but I just happened to be the one to get hurt. And both of us didn't do any more than each of you would have done for us if you'd been in our shoes."

While the boys played with the racing set, Sylvia and Francine sat in the middle of the living-room floor, the other girls in a circle around them, and taught the younger girls some folk songs. Then they switched to popular songs, and ended with a Christmas carol and a Yiddish lullaby. Sylvia sang the words to that as the rest of them hummed the melody.

Audrey, sitting next to Hope, kept stealing glances at her friend, who sang with so much enthusiasm. Audrey felt a thrill of satisfaction about everything: the Chanukah party, the activities of their club, her friendship with Hope, and — yes, her friendship with all these other girls! As she glanced from face to glowing face, she realized with sharp surprise that, truly, they *were* wonderful, just as wonderful as her friends back in New York. They were very different, and that had taken some getting used to. But then, Audrey thought, she also was different to them. Yet they had accepted her right away — and gradually they were accepting new and different ideas too.

After the last song, the girls stretched and yawned, looking as relaxed and happy as cats after a full saucer of milk.

"This is the best party I've been to in a long time," Lorraine said.

"It's the best Chanukah party I've ever been to in my life!" Patsy said, as the others added, laughing with her, "And the *only* one!"

"Well, I hope it's only the first of many," Sylvia said. "It was even more fun for us to have you, especially since it was your first. Oh, that reminds me —" She jumped up and hurried into the kitchen, returning in moments with a big box. "These are for you to remember tonight by." She handed each girl a red plastic dreidel stamped with gold Hebrew letters and filled with little presents — hair bows, tiny ballpoint pens, nail brushes, and shiny gold thimbles.

"Well, what do you know," Audrey remarked. "Jewish activity boxes!"

Everyone screamed with laughter, and suddenly five little-boy faces appeared.

"Hey, what's going on up here?"

"Don't worry, we have one for each of you too." Sylvia handed them each a blue dreidel filled with miniature tools and bubble gum.

She shook her head as they all exclaimed over their gifts, telling them: "Don't thank me — I didn't know anything about it. There's the lady responsible for everything." And she nodded at her mother, who stood smiling near her.

Everyone crowded around to say thank you, and soon the Goldberg family was standing at the outside door, waving to their young guests as they trooped down the walk, calling back their final good wishes for a happy Chanukah.

As they turned toward home, Rosie linked one arm through Audrey's and the other through Hope's and exclaimed, "Say, do you know something? We never *did* learn to dance at that party! In fact, we never did finish the party!"

"Why, we never even had a chance to *eat*," Doris said.

"Well, you could say we made up for that tonight," Patsy told her.

"We'll just have to pick up where we left off — maybe when Christmas vacation starts. And at our January meeting, we'll have to plan what project to work on next," Joan said.

"Do you know what?" Audrey smiled as she spoke. "I think I like Jupiter just as much as New York."

"Is that all?" Lorraine said, disappointed. Then she shrugged. "Well, by summer vacation, I'll bet you'll like it even *better*."

"Do you know what?" Audrey repeated. "I bet you're right!"